SHIVER POINT

IT CAME FROM THE WOODS

SHIVER POINT

IT CAME FROM THE WOODS

GABRIEL DYLAN

Piccadilly
PRESS

First published in Great Britain in 2023 by
PICCADILLY PRESS
4th Floor, Victoria House, Bloomsbury Square
London WC1B 4DA
Owned by Bonnier Books
Sveavägen 56, Stockholm, Sweden
bonnierbooks.co.uk/PiccadillyPress

A CIP catalogue record for this book is available from the
British Library.

ISBN: 978-1-80078-477-2
Also available as an ebook and in audio

1

Typeset by Data Connection
Printed and bound in Great Britain by Clays Ltd, Elcograf S.p.A.

Piccadilly Press is an imprint of Bonnier Books UK
bonnierbooks.co.uk

To Mum and Dad

For always being there

And for letting me stay up late to watch all those scary films when I was little

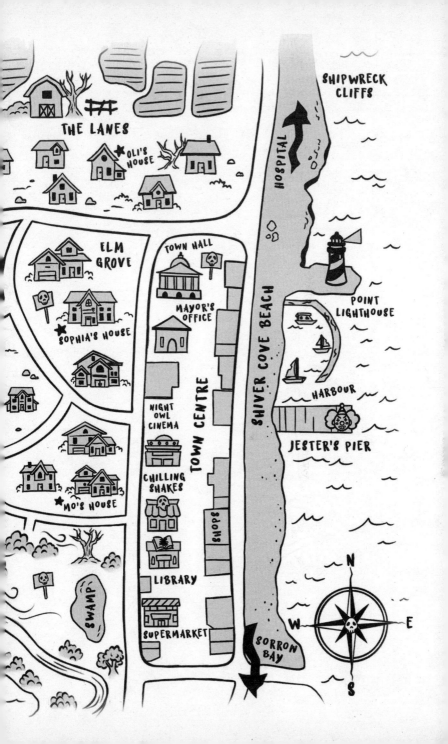

1

I SAW IT FIRST

The light in the sky had come down somewhere in the trees.

The problem was that those trees were part of Howlmoor Forest.

Alex had been on his skateboard, cruising back and forth on the tatty halfpipe he'd built in his mum's tiny back garden, when he'd seen the light burst through the clouds. At first he'd thought it was a plane, jetting through the night sky to somewhere far more exciting than Shiver Point, or a firework set off on the other side of town, but he'd quickly changed his mind. It was too fast for a plane and too bright to be a firework. An odd sense of dread washed over Alex, a strange feeling that the light up in the sky wasn't quite normal.

A heartbeat later it was gone. The glow sank towards the horizon, vanishing into the dark mass of the forest with a curious green flash. Alex rubbed at his eyes to check he wasn't dreaming, and glanced down at his watch.

Five minutes past midnight, and still no sign of his mum.

This was the way life had been since they had moved to Shiver Point a few months ago. His mum's shifts at the hospital were running later and later, and Alex found himself staying up hours past his bedtime to see her when she got home.

He fought back a yawn, studying the distant trees once more. Had there *really* been something in the sky?

Suddenly a memory popped into Alex's brain, the voice of his geography teacher, Mr Williams, delivering pretty much the only interesting lesson he'd taught all term. The topic of the lesson had been meteors, and one of the class had asked the teacher if a lump of space rock would be valuable.

'I'd imagine so,' Mr Williams had said, staring up at the classroom ceiling as if a fiery meteorite was about to smash through the tiles and make a big runny mess of several of Alex's classmates. 'They're rare, but sometimes they do come down, in which case they're called *meteorites*. If you found a piece of one, you might get a few thousand pounds for it at an auction.'

The teacher's answer had drawn a series of gasps and mutters from the class, most of them probably wondering how many milkshakes they could get from Chilling Shakes, Shiver Point's premier cafe, with that much cash, and if it was possible to buy your way out of having to go to school. As the other pupils had huddled together, excitedly planning their purchases, Alex had known exactly how he'd spend that kind of money.

A few minutes later the bell had gone, ending the discussion. While the rest of the class had scrambled outside, heading off to lunchtime clubs or to kick a ball around the field, Alex had been the last to leave. It wasn't the fact that he still hadn't made any friends in Shiver Point, or that he spent every lunchtime and break on his own. No, he was daydreaming about how finding something like a meteor could turn things around for him and his mum.

The memory faded away and Alex turned his attention back towards Howlmoor Forest. The woodlands stretched on for *miles*, and he wasn't convinced that stumbling around in the darkness, losing his way and getting freaked out until morning, was the best idea he'd ever had. But . . . what if that thing from the sky turned out to be worth a lot of money?

Before Alex had time to think things through any further he had vaulted the garden fence, leaped onto his skateboard and was tearing towards town. When his mum was at work she asked the old lady next door, Alison, to keep an eye on Alex, but he was pretty sure she'd never seen him sneak out. Not that he did it much. Well, not very much. Anyway, the one time Alex *had* needed her, when he'd set the toaster on fire, Alison had been fast asleep in her chair in front of *Antiques Roadshow*, impossible to rouse no matter how hard Alex hammered on the door.

Shiver Point was deserted, the only noise the rattle of Alex's skateboard and the screech of his wheels whenever he turned a corner. The streets took on a haunted edge at this time of night, the darkened windows seeming to glare as Alex flew past, the shadows beyond the street lights groping towards him. He felt a shiver of fright as he realised how alone he was, and made his skateboard go a little bit quicker.

He soared past Point Academy, scowling in the school's direction, then crouched lower as he gained speed downhill, the scruffy houses of their neighbourhood giving way to the bigger, more expensive properties of Elm Grove, with their plush gardens and manicured lawns. Shiver Point wasn't big, and that was part of Alex's problem with the town; there was no mall, no skate park and hardly any coffee shops or fast-food joints to hang out in, like he used to do with his friends back home. Kids in his class went on about Chilling Shakes on the high street, or its neighbour the Night Owl Cinema, but neither was worth the fuss. From Alex's experience, the milkshakes really weren't all that special, and the only films the Night Owl showed were ancient. Moving here had been like going back in time, to an era before Netflix and YouTube came into the world.

Alex was approaching the seafront now, the cries of the gulls echoing mournfully through the darkness. His mum had made a big deal about how great it would be living by the seaside, but even that was a disappointment. The pier was grey and dull, a layer of rust covering the abandoned rides and amusements, and the ocean was a murky brown. If Alex had his way he'd have kept on skating until he left Shiver Point far behind. But maybe, just maybe, what he'd seen in the sky would give him another escape route . . .

It was less than fifteen minutes before Alex found the town streets morphing into country lanes, the yellow glare of the streetlights replaced by the shadows that loomed at the edge of Howlmoor Forest. As he screeched to a stop and peered into the dark expanse of woodland, he wasn't sure his plan was so great after all. He didn't believe in ghosts and ghouls and things

6

that went bump in the night, but he wasn't totally thrilled at the idea of venturing into the woods either. Alex had never liked forests, not since his mum had read him the story of Hansel and Gretel, and he couldn't shake the idea that hidden eyes might be watching him from the gloom, just waiting to pounce and drag him screaming to a creepy cabin deep in the woods.

It was only the thought of his mum, and how things had been lately, that made him pick up his board and push his way into the trees. Since they'd moved to Shiver Point it felt like Alex barely saw his mum; she seemed to spend more time with her patients than she ever did with him. And when she wasn't tired from working nights, she was moody and snappish, and didn't respond well to Alex's complaints about how dull Shiver Point was. She used to be his best friend, only recently it felt like she was a stranger, and a grumpy one at that.

But a sudden influx of cash from a chunk of space rock would change *everything*. Alex pictured the auction hall, the sound of the hammer crashing down as his find sold for thousands. His mum would get a job where he actually saw her, the two of them would move back to their old home, to Alex's friends, to the way things were before . . .

Or at least that was what Alex tried to convince himself of as the trees closed in around him. The further he crept on, the more menacing things became. The trees blocked out the moonlight, banishing Shiver Point from view and concealing everything in shadows. Gnarled branches groped at Alex's clothes and dragged cobwebs over his face, and leaves tickled against the collar of his shirt like spiders. The whispers and rustles of tiny creatures in the undergrowth were magnified by the darkness. Alex told himself it was just his imagination, but he was sure that at any moment he'd feel cold breath on the back of his neck and bony fingers biting into his wrists.

He held his skateboard in front of him like a shield and forced himself to put one foot in front of the other.

He wished he wasn't on his own.

He wished he'd brought a torch.

But more than anything, he wished he'd gone to the toilet before he left home.

Alex had been creeping through the woods for what felt like forever when he came to the conclusion that he was in serious danger of getting lost and that his get-rich-quick scheme had crashed and burned.

'What am I doing?' he whispered to himself, wincing in fright at how loud his words sounded. 'Do I want to end up on a Missing poster pinned up in the school hallway?'

He was just about to turn around and try to find his way back to the road when something caught his eye – a glimmer of light in the distance. He paused, his pulse starting to throb in his temples. It was green, just like the light in the sky . . . and that could only mean one thing.

He'd found where the light had come down!

Alex quickened his pace, pushing his way through the trees, no longer caring how much noise he made. As he grew closer, though, confusion washed over him. There was a clearing up ahead, a space where the trees didn't grow, but it looked as if a group of figures stood there, staring into the light.

The disappointment hit Alex like a sledgehammer. Someone else had got to the crash site first! Alex powered forward anyway, his excitement replaced by anger that any chance of transforming his life was fading away. But when he burst into the open and saw what the others were looking at, all Alex could do was stare too.

If there were any doubts in his mind that what he'd seen in the sky had just been his imagination, they quickly faded. Dozens of pieces of charred, jagged rock sat in the middle of the clearing, the grass around them scorched and blackened. Each chunk gave off a bright green shimmer, reminding Alex of the luminous radioactive waste he'd seen in science-fiction films. A series of gooey black splodges dotted the burnt ground, like splats of sludgy oil.

'What . . . what happened?' Alex heard himself ask, making the figures jump at the sound of the voice that had crept up on them.

They spun to face him and he squinted at their faces, realising that he vaguely recognised them all from Point Academy.

'It's a meteor, or at least it was,' replied a neat-looking blonde girl Alex recognised as Sophia Smith. She was in Alex's English class and seemed to know everything about everything, except how to get along with people. 'You know, a piece of rock or matter from outer space that drifts through the universe, looking for a planet to collide with.'

'Aren't meteors dangerous? Didn't they, like, kill the dinosaurs?'

The words came from the mouth of a tall boy with a gap-toothed smile. Alex didn't know Oli Foster that well, but then it was hard to know someone who spent so much time in the Cooler, Point Academy's detention block for disruptive pupils. Despite the danger of the situation Oli seemed unfazed by it all, scratching at his curly hair as he stared at the crash site.

'Duh, that was an asteroid, not a meteorite,' hissed Sophia, taking a step towards the rocks, then thinking better of it when one of the chunks crackled and hissed, as if it was still sizzling from burning its way through the atmosphere. 'And if it was going to kill us, we'd be squashed already – us and the whole town. The one that killed the dinosaurs was six miles wide and sent up so much dust it blocked out the sun.'

'OK, Little Miss Wikipedia,' Oli fired back. 'If I wanted a science lesson, I'd have listened in class.'

'Don't you usually get thrown out of class?' Sophia murmured under her breath.

'What are you all doing here?' Alex interrupted, wondering if there was some way he could persuade them to get lost and let him have the rocks. The meteorite was his – he'd seen it first and he was pretty sure he needed the money a lot more than they did.

'I was up late, reading about osmosis before tomorrow's science lesson,' Sophia announced proudly, like she expected Alex to pin an achievement badge on the lapel of her blazer as a reward for the work she'd put in.

'I was at my telescope,' exclaimed a short boy with a beanie on his head and a set of binoculars on a string around his neck. 'I'd heard there was going to be a meteor shower and I've been looking forward to it all week.'

Alex had only ever spoken to Mo Bhaiyat once before, when they'd both forgotten their PE kit. As punishment, Mr Brown had forced them to pick the used gum from underneath the tables in his classroom, one foul, squishy lump at a time. While Alex had kept his head down and tried to get through the gum torture as quickly as he could, Mo had spent the time babbling on about the birdwatching club he was setting up at the school and explaining how he was looking for new members, an invitation Alex very much avoided.

Oli looked at Mo like he'd just admitted to sucking his thumb. 'I was up late, fragging aliens on my Xbox, trying to stay king of the leader board. When I saw that thing in the sky I thought I'd been sucked into the game, like in those Jumanji films.'

The last member of the group had a set of goggles on her head, like a mad scientist or a Ghostbuster. Alex was pretty sure her name was Riley Ogunleye and that she lived in a creepy old cottage right next to Shadow Hill cemetery. He'd skated past there sometimes and seen her vanishing through the gate once or twice, but other than that she was a mystery.

A crash from deeper in the woods made them all spin round. Despite the torches the others had all been organised enough to bring, it was still impossible to see more than a few metres ahead: the thick wall of trees circling the clearing looked impenetrable.

'Maybe we should go,' stuttered Mo, his eyes wide behind the thick lenses of his glasses. 'I haven't been this scared since Bethany Blight hid that false widow spider in my lunch box.'

Alex shivered at the mention of Bethany Blight. Most of the kids at Point Academy seemed pleasant enough, but not Bethany. He'd met bullies before, but none quite as bad.

Riley turned back to the crash site, seemingly unflustered, and slid the strange goggles down over her eyes to study the black slime on the ground.

'It looks like some kind of liquid,' she mused. 'But where did it come from?'

Another noise came from somewhere in the trees, sounding like the crack of something heavy coming down on a fallen branch.

Mo let out a shrill whine, like a hiss of air being let out of a balloon. 'You think . . . that someone else has found the crash site too? Or could it be a boar? I've heard they come out in Howlmoor after dark, looking for lost hikers to trample.'

Sophia rolled her eyes, pulling a small notebook out of her pocket. 'Are there any forest-dwelling creatures you're *not* scared of? The Gruffalo? Peppa Pig? I think we need to –'

Nobody heard the rest of what Sophia had to say. The words were drowned out by a chilling, high-pitched shriek, echoing through the trees like a banshee's wail. Alex had no idea what could make a sound like that, and he didn't want to find out.

'Please tell me that was someone's stomach,' he breathed, trying his best to keep the jitter from his voice but not quite succeeding.

'Dude, my stomach hasn't ever made that kind of noise, not even when I ate three of those disgusting vegan hot dogs from the canteen,' replied Oli, arming himself with a large stick from the ground.

As Alex glanced around the trees edging their little clearing, his eye caught a movement. Just there . . . a thin, dark shadow, creeping through the undergrowth, moving in their direction.

'Guys?' he whispered.

The others turned to face him, torch beams piercing the shadows.

Alex's heartbeat started to hammer in his chest. 'Hello?' he called. 'Is there somebody else out there?'

'What do we do?' whispered Mo, the torch in his hand trembling as if there was an earthquake.

Alex squinted, trying to get a better look at the silhouette, and caught a hint of something pale glinting in the moonlight. *Teeth*, whispered a voice deep in Alex's mind. *All the better to eat you with.*

'What do we do?' Mo asked again, louder this time.

This time Alex didn't need to think about the answer at all.

'Run!'

2
DON'T PANIC

Maybe the shape in the trees was a trick of the light.

Maybe it was just that weird phenomenon when one person runs and everyone else does too, like when two people have beef at school and suddenly there's a whole stampede of frantic kids desperate to find out what's happening.

Whatever it was, one minute Alex and the others were standing there, peering into the trees, the next they were racing back the way they'd come. In a second, the forest air filled with yells and screams, everyone trying not to rip their clothes or break an ankle on a tree root

17

as they scrambled through the darkness, the beams from their torches darting left and right as they ran, like lasers at a pop concert.

Alex wasn't sure what he'd seen, but he didn't intend to hang around long enough to find out. Even as he ran, his skateboard knocking against his legs and trying to trip him up, the sensible part of Alex's mind started to slide back into control, reminding him that there was no such thing as monsters, and that between the darkness and the shadows there was a chance he hadn't seen anything at all. He wanted to stop, but at the same time he didn't want to lose the others, especially as they all had torches and he didn't.

Alex's legs were just reaching the point where he wasn't sure if he could go on when Mo vanished. One second he was there, sprinting alongside them all, a look of wild panic in his eyes, the next he was gone. It was as if someone had clicked their fingers Thanos-style and turned him to dust.

Alex skidded to a halt, turned around frantically and tried to work out where Mo could have gone. Alex had only been at Point Academy a few months, but he'd seen enough of Mo to figure him out already. Mo was one of life's victims, the kind of kid whose drink bottle was always leaking in his bag and who constantly got told off for being late to lessons because he could never find the right classroom. But even if Mo wasn't the most popular kid at school, Alex knew he couldn't just leave him behind. He turned back the way he'd come, desperately searching the shadows for any sign of the boy. He was relieved to see Riley scrambling alongside him, scanning the area with those weird goggles of hers, which by now Alex was fairly sure must be somehow allowing her to see in the dark.

'There!' she announced, jabbing her finger in the direction of a clump of fallen leaves. Two arms and two legs poked out, wiggling desperately like a turtle stuck on its back.

Oli barrelled past Alex and Riley and yanked Mo back to his feet, pushing him onwards so forcefully that the smaller boy nearly went flying again.

'Come on, slowcoach, let's go!' Oli yelled.

'Which . . . which way is it?' Mo asked, digging into his pocket and pulling out his phone. A puzzled look slid over Oli's face. Now that Alex thought about it, he wasn't sure which way led out of the forest either. He'd been so intent on finding the crash site that he hadn't given enough thought to getting back home. He felt a jolt of panic as he studied the shadows and realised that every direction looked distressingly similar.

Trees.

Lots and lots of trees.

'What are you doing just standing around?' demanded Sophia, who'd pressed ahead without them but clearly hadn't got very far and had decided to double back to join them. She brushed the leaves from her blazer, straightening the *prefect* badge she had pinned to the lapel, although Alex couldn't work out why anyone would be wearing their school uniform at midnight.

'I'm checking Google Maps,' Mo replied, holding his phone up in the air in that dumb way adults did when they couldn't get a signal.

'Are you for real?' Oli asked, the look on his face suggesting that he was starting to regret helping Mo back to his feet.

'There's never any signal in Howlmoor,' Sophia snapped, snatching Mo's phone off him and clicking the screen off. 'Right now what we need to do is follow the stars.'

'What do you mean, follow the stars?' asked Oli. 'Are they, like, on Instagram or Snapchat?'

Sophia took a deep, patient breath. 'I mean we need to look up at the stars, because no matter where you are, you can use the stars to guide you. We need to head north-east. So we need to find the North Star and from that we can work out which direction to head in.'

Alex did the same as everyone else, tilting his head to peer up through the trees, but apart from the clouds and the odd bat that flew by there wasn't much to see.

'It's cloudy,' squealed Mo. 'What do we do now?'

Alex held up his hand for quiet. 'Listen, guys, the important thing is that we don't –'

He was about to finish his sentence with 'panic', but another shriek from somewhere in the darkness killed the word in his throat. There were other sounds too, something trampling through the undergrowth not far from where they'd paused. Alex wasn't one to scare easily, but suddenly his teeth were chattering like a typewriter.

'Go!' he yelled, abandoning whatever plan he'd been trying to come up with and breaking into a dash through the darkness.

No one argued.

Riley elbowed her way to the front of their group, using her goggles to scout the way ahead and shouting a warning whenever a branch or tree root jutted into their path. Alex felt a surge of relief when he finally caught a glimmer of open space in the distance.

'That way!' he called. 'Almost there!'

A few seconds later they burst out into the open by the road. Alex came to a stop, his breath a hot poker in his chest, his legs weak and wobbly. He wiped the sweat from his forehead, scanning the others' frightened faces.

'Did that . . . did that really happen?' whispered Mo.

For a few seconds everyone was too out of breath to respond. Oli broke into a high-pitched giggle, like he'd been chased by Bethany Blight and managed to get away. Just as Alex opened his mouth to say – mainly to reassure himself – that the whole thing had been some dumb misunderstanding, another muted wail drifted through the night, echoing from within the trees. They might have made it out of Howlmoor, but whatever they'd heard was still prowling around, and getting closer from the sound of it. Any last thoughts of meteors or auctions evacuated Alex's brain, replaced by a sudden need to get back home, lock the door and switch on the brightest light he could find.

Evidently the others felt the same way. Mo was already almost out of sight, Oli's grin was fading fast, and Riley and Sophia were backing away from the trees, moving towards a pair of bicycles stashed in the undergrowth.

Alex didn't bother to say goodbye. He dropped his skateboard on the tarmac, jumped on and sped home as quickly as he could.

3

ODD ONE OUT

Mo plodded along the street, lost in his own world as his feet steered him on autopilot towards school. It was only eight thirty in the morning, but he could already sense it was going to be a bad day. His dog, Pluto, had eaten the science homework that was due in first lesson, and his Minecraft flask had leaked in his bag the moment he'd placed it inside, contaminating the akhni he had for lunch. Not only was he going to get a detention for the homework from Mrs Taylor, but his rice was going to be even soggier than normal.

But despite his problems, all Mo could focus on was what had happened three nights ago.

Mo had been excited about the meteor shower since he'd seen the forecast on the internet. For a junior astronomer like him, it was a dream come true. He'd got his Celestron Astromaster telescope for his tenth birthday and he'd used it almost every night in the two years since. On a clear night he could see as far as the rings of Saturn and the moons of Jupiter, and to stars and planets light years away from his messy bedroom. As he'd got older, Mo's telescope had become an escape from the noise and chaos of home, from his mum making him help out in the kitchen, from his annoying little brother, Zunaid, who was always pestering him. More than that though, Mo was fascinated by the endless galaxies with their distant constellations. He loved the thought of alien civilisations, millions of miles away, staring back at him through their own telescopes.

That didn't mean he wanted to meet them though.

Especially not if they looked like that weird shape he'd seen in Howlmoor Forest.

Of course what they'd seen in the forest that night wasn't an alien. That would be ridiculous. But whatever it had been, Mo wasn't willing to hang around to find out. He'd made the sprint from Howlmoor back to his house in record time, crept into the bedroom he shared with his brother and hidden under the blankets for the rest of the night.

The whole episode was like a bad dream, except Mo knew from the rips in his trousers and his muddy shoes that it was real. But had there been some*one* or some*thing* in the woods that night?

A car horn bellowed down the street, snapping Mo out of his daydreams. He looked up, saw that he was at the school gates and tried to focus on the lessons he had today. That had been the other strange thing about the woods that night – the fact that four other kids from Point Academy had been there too.

An idea suddenly occurred to Mo. Maybe he should try to talk to Alex and the others, find out what they made of it all. They'd all had a few days to mull on it – they might have thought of something he hadn't. And it might even earn him a friend or two, something that was distinctly lacking from his time at school.

He went looking for Riley first. She wasn't friendly exactly, but Mo thought she seemed like the least unfriendly of the group. He found her at first break, working in the DT lab on a mass of wires and metal that looked suspiciously like some kind of robot. Mo barely knew her, but he did know that she was something of an expert when it came to electronics and engineering. The teacher, Mrs Sewell, was in the corner of the room, messing with a welding kit, so Mo lingered by the door, trying to catch Riley's eye.

It didn't take long for her to spot him. But rather than give him a smile and a wave, Riley's face went pale and she focused even harder on whatever she was working on without so much as saying hello.

Mo was disappointed but determined to speak to someone, so he tried Oli next. He found him hanging out by the lockers with some kids from the year above, who were taking huge gulps of fizzy drink and then seeing who could produce the loudest burp. The echoing belches were what alerted Mo to their location, sounding down the corridor like a siren. This time Mo tried waving, but Oli jumped when he saw him, the burp he was midway through producing becoming more of a squeal. Startled by Oli's reaction, Mo scurried off and decided to try someone else.

His third stop was the tuck shop, where Sophia worked as a prefect during break times. Sophia was someone Mo couldn't quite work out how to deal with. In some ways the two of them were quite similar, with a shared love of science and learning, but sometimes, when they worked together in lessons, she'd just huff at Mo, as if none of his ideas were quite as good as her own.

Bracing himself, Mo went up to the counter, where she was measuring out a portion of flying saucers, but the moment she saw him the spoon in her hand started to shake, and she moved away from the till without a word. It seemed like all the others were just as disturbed as he was about what had happened in the forest.

Alex was the last one Mo caught up with, five minutes before the bell was due to ring for next lesson. He was sitting on the steps at the front of Point Academy, a sketchbook open in his lap as he stared at the horizon.

Mo still wasn't sure what to make of Alex. He'd only been at Point Academy for a few months, and he barely spoke to anyone, keeping his head down in lessons and never getting involved unless he was forced to. He always wore a scruffy hoodie under his blazer and arrived at school on his skateboard just in time for registration. Mo wasn't sure if Alex was really shy or just thought he was too cool to talk to anyone else.

Maybe it was time to find out.

Mo cleared his throat, edging a step closer. 'Hey, Alex. What are you drawing?'

Alex jumped at the words, almost ripping a hole in the page with the tip of his pencil. Mo looked down, realising that Alex had been drawing what looked like Howlmoor Forest, the huge clump of green visible in the distance that Alex had been staring at when Mo approached. Alex caught him looking at the picture and slammed his sketchbook shut.

'Erm . . . nothing.'

Mo shifted uncomfortably from one foot to the other, trying not to look as if he needed the toilet. 'Look, I'm sorry to interrupt your drawing, but I wanted to talk to someone, and . . .'

Mo wasn't sure how to go on. Now that he thought about it, the whole thing sounded stupid. The best thing to do, he reckoned, was to just come out and say it.

'I think that maybe we weren't alone in the forest the other night.'

Alex stared at him for a few seconds, as if the gears in his head were slowly turning.

'It was just us,' he finally answered. 'We just got freaked out by the shadows, and that huge chunk of rock that had come down.'

Mo shook his head, picturing the eerie forest, the screeching noise that had ripped through the trees. 'But what about that noise we heard?'

Alex climbed to his feet, stuffing his sketchbook into his bag. 'It was probably just an owl, or something caught by a fox.' The look on his face suggested he didn't really believe what he was saying either.

Mo opened his mouth to ask Alex if owls were different where he came from, but he never got the chance.

'Whatever it was, I won't be going near the place again,' Alex continued. 'I ripped a hole in my trainers, and nearly poked my eye out on a branch. Look, I've got to go. I'll see you around.' He started to move in the direction of the art bay.

The words were out of Mo's mouth before he could stop them. 'Hey, you're still pretty new here, and you always seem to be on your own. Want to . . . want to hang out sometime?'

The question seemed to catch Alex by surprise, and he froze, a conflicted expression sliding over his face.

'Thanks,' he muttered. 'But no. I just . . . I just prefer it on my own now.'

And with that he was gone.

Mo tried to ignore the disappointment settling in his chest. Today was clearly not the day he'd finally make any friends.

Alex was probably right about the forest though, and the whole thing had likely been nothing but Mo's imagination. Either way, it seemed as if the rest of the kids who had been there that night just wanted to forget about it. The problem was, Mo didn't think he'd be able to ignore it quite as easily as the others, especially that sound they'd heard, which had taken on a starring role in his nightmares over the past few nights.

Mo's next lesson was science, but despite it being his favourite subject, his day didn't get any better. As well as earning a detention for the homework, Mo found himself sitting in front of Bethany Blight. She had a habit of choosing someone to pick on each lesson and making their life a misery. Today it was Mo's turn. It seemed to be Mo's turn more than anyone else's.

Every time Miss Newman looked away, Bethany fired a sticky lump of chewed-up paper through a straw she'd taken from the canteen, right at Mo's head. It was like being assaulted by a swarm of soggy mosquitos, again and again.

But at least *someone* noticed him, thought Mo.

4

SLUG SURPRISE

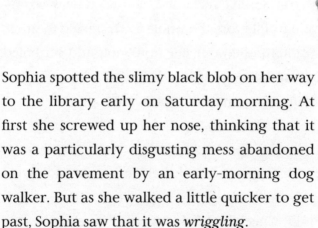

Sophia spotted the slimy black blob on her way to the library early on Saturday morning. At first she screwed up her nose, thinking that it was a particularly disgusting mess abandoned on the pavement by an early-morning dog walker. But as she walked a little quicker to get past, Sophia saw that it was *wriggling*.

Never one to pass up on a learning opportunity, Sophia came to a halt, her eyes drawn towards the weird shape at the edge of the kerb. She leaned closer, fighting a wave of revulsion as the odd shape slithered in the direction of the drain, leaving a shiny black trail. It sort of resembled a slug, Sophia realised, some weird, three-eyed, exotic variety that looked like it was from the depths of outer space. But it was too big to be a slug, too slimy, too . . . revolting.

Now that Sophia had stopped, she noticed something else. An awful smell hung in the air, not just from the writhing black shape, but from the drain it was desperately trying to slither towards. Someone needed to get down there, Sophia reckoned, see what was wrong and fix it before the whole town started to smell. Sophia pulled out her notebook and scribbled a reminder on her to-do list to tell one of her mums as soon as she got home.

To do:
- ☐ Organise bookshelf into chronological order
- ☐ Check highlighters are all working
- ☐ Polish prefect and librarian badges
- ☐ Speak to Mummy and Mum about the drains

As Sophia was slipping the notebook back into her pocket, the clouds above parted, a beam of sun bursting through. Sophia looked up, enjoying the warmth on her face, but a loud popping noise made her jump. The yucky creature down by her feet had burst open, like a bag of popcorn left too long in the microwave. Sophia put a hand to her mouth as the slug shrivelled and writhed.

She'd never seen anything like it before.

A postman trotted past, gave Sophia a curious stare from underneath his bushy eyebrows and vanished up a nearby driveway. Suddenly Sophia realised how stupid she must look, standing there staring at a dying slug. She wanted to explain to the postman that it wasn't a slug at all, or to walk away and not give it another thought, but there was something odd about the small black creature, something strangely familiar. She leaned closer, studying the gooey mess.

And then it came to her.

The pool of black slime was just the same as the one she'd seen in Howlmoor Forest, right after she'd stumbled across where the meteorite had come down. She'd been trying ever since not to think about that night, even when Mo had come to talk to her the other day at school. Maybe she should have spoken to him, even just said hello, but the truth was that the whole episode had scared Sophia, and it was something she'd rather forget, even if she was a little intrigued by what they'd all seen. Besides, Sophia found she worked best alone, and she wasn't all that interested in working with other people, unless you counted the town librarian, Ms Stoker, which she supposed you couldn't really.

Sophia took a deep breath and stepped away from the drain. Surely the resemblance between the small slimy creature and that goo in the woods was just a coincidence. Anyway, she had far more important things to do than stare at some freaky slug that wasn't a slug. It was almost gone now, reduced to a small black puddle on the pavement. If Sophia hadn't been in Shiver Point, she might have thought there was something weird about it, but nothing exciting *ever* happened in Shiver Point.

Sophia set off in the direction of town again, quicker now. She volunteered every Saturday in the Shiver Point library, and if she didn't get a move on she was going to be late, which wouldn't look good.

Sophia was never late, not for anything.

As she walked, she pulled out her notebook again, scribbling down another reminder. Even though she was ninety-nine per cent sure there was nothing to it, she decided that while she was in the library today she was going to do a little research into slugs – odd, smelly ones that were twice their normal size. Sophia didn't like it when things didn't make sense, and the dissolving slug was one mystery she was determined to solve.

5

SOMETHING BAD

There was something going on in Shiver Point.

Something *bad*.

Maybe Oli hardly ever got things right at school, but this time he knew he was right. He wasn't too good at English, science or maths, but if there was ever a test on horror films, he knew he'd beat the rest of the class hands down.

Oli loved horror films. He wasn't really allowed to watch them, not at his age, but the one benefit of having two older sisters was being able to borrow their stuff: their hoodies, phone chargers, headphones.

And their films.

Oli's oldest sister, Cassie, had a whole wall full of old horror DVDs, bought for next to nothing from the local charity shop, and Oli had watched all of them. He knew how to spot the signs of a poltergeist haunting, or a zombie apocalypse, or a vampire infestation. He knew how to deal with a killer clown that could shapeshift into a spider, or an exotic cuddly pet that would turn into a murderous gremlin if it ate after midnight.

And standing in the supermarket, staring at the empty shelves, Oli had the strongest sense that things weren't quite right in Shiver Point.

From what he could gather, someone had broken into the shop overnight. In case the shattered glass left any doubt, the notice pinned onto the store's front door made it clear.

> *Due to last night's break-in, some of our*
> *products are out of stock.*
> *Thanks for your patience.*

At first Oli wondered what had been taken, but as he stood staring at the empty shelves where the cat food should have been, he realised that the answer was right in front of him.

'What kind of weirdo steals all the cat food?' he asked aloud, earning a curious look from a lady struggling with a wayward trolley as she squeaked by. But the missing cat food was just one in a series of odd things that had happened in Shiver Point over the past week.

First there had been that freaky chunk of rock that had crashed down in Howlmoor, and the weird shrieks that had chased Oli and the others out of the forest. Then there had been the way the internet kept going down across the town, costing Oli his place on the top of the *Deadshot* leader board when his router had failed during a particularly intense shoot-out. Phones seemed equally patchy, with Oli's other sister, Sara, getting so enraged at being unable to text her boyfriend that she'd dropped her phone down the toilet. Then there was the odd smell that seemed to have drifted from the forest and was now hanging over Shiver Point like a cloud. And the weird, familiar black splodges Oli had spotted by the supermarket doors near where the break-in had happened. If Oli didn't know better, and if Shiver Point wasn't so bone-crushingly dull, he'd say it was all connected.

Maybe he was the only one that had noticed the strange mood that hung over the town. Or maybe his vast knowledge of horror films had finally got the better of him and pushed his vivid imagination into overdrive. Either way, Cujo his pet cat was going hungry tonight.

Oli left the cat-food aisle, got the rest of the groceries that his mum had asked him to pick up and stumbled outside. That was the problem with being the middle child – he was always the one that got given the boring jobs because everyone else had more important things to do. Cassie and Sara were too busy with exams to get sent to the shop, and Oli's little sister, Thea, was too young for the task. So as usual it was Oli who was sent to the supermarket whenever they ran out of things, which seemed to happen a little too often.

He was about to head home when he noticed a crowd of people who'd stopped to chat to one of the reporters from the local newspaper, the *Shivering Post*. Oli knew the reporter, Damian Thorn, well enough. He was always hanging around town, that little microphone in his hand, whenever there was anything vaguely interesting going on, his beady eyes drawn towards Oli as if whatever had happened was his fault. The most frustrating thing was, Oli never meant to cause any kind of trouble. He knew he was loud, and bigger than the other kids his age, and easily distracted, but he never meant to cause problems, they just kind of happened. Like the time he'd set the mice free in the science labs and caused an infestation. Or the time he'd lit the fireworks on the school field and set fire to the stands.

At least Thorn finally had something serious to report now, with all the weird things happening in Shiver Point, but Oli reckoned the reporter wasn't clever enough to put the pieces together. Nobody would ever expect it, but this time Oli was the one who might just have all the answers. He edged away, a cold shudder running down his spine. He tried to tell himself that he was imagining things, that he was being stupid, but the feeling followed him all the way home like a severed hand slowly crawling after him.

Something was going on in Shiver Point.

Something bad.

6

SCHOOL'S OUT

The great thing about computers was that they always made sense. They didn't care if you'd had a bad day, or weren't in the mood to chat. They didn't ask awkward questions about why you lived in the creepy house next to Shadow Hill cemetery, or why you had no mum or dad. They just did what they were told.

Maybe that was why Riley liked ICT so much.

Except today the lesson wasn't going to be happening. There'd been a weird mood at Point Academy since the moment Riley had trudged into her tutor room. From what she could gather, three teachers had called in sick today, and that meant some lessons were going to end up being cancelled and cover work set instead. By the time the bell rang and Riley made her way to her first class, it looked as if ICT was going to be the first of those casualties. The classroom was locked, the lights were out and a queue of bored-looking pupils were muttering in the corridor.

Riley placed herself at the back of the line, pulling out her phone to check the time.

And that was when Oli caught her eye.

Riley remembered the last time she'd spoken to Oli all too well, so well that whenever she thought of it she got all freaked out. She'd always had a problem sleeping, and inventing stuff in her den – taking pieces of junk that no one else wanted and making them into something new – took her mind off her problems. When she'd seen the light come down, she'd known it would be the ideal test for her latest invention, and she'd been right. On the way into the forest, Riley's night-vision goggles had lit the route perfectly. She'd made them using an old pair of sunglasses, a battered analogue camera and a handful of batteries. Except when she'd seen that

44

weird shape moving in the trees, she'd wondered if they were faulty. And then she'd decided it didn't matter and the most important thing was to get out of there and home to her grandad.

Footsteps stamped down the corridor, snapping Riley back to the present. Mr Drumm slipped into view, his long, grey-streaked hair tied back in a ponytail. He was wearing his crumpled beige suit, the one that made him look as if he'd just traipsed across the Sahara or hacked his way through a jungle.

'Sorry, class,' he sputtered, pulling a set of keys out of his jacket pocket. 'I'm running a little late this morning.'

The teacher fumbled his keys into the lock and began to usher the groggy pupils inside, until they all stopped abruptly. Riley stretched up onto her tiptoes to see what had caused the hold-up just as a loud collective gasp sounded from the front of the group of students. Shouldering her way into the classroom, Riley skidded to a halt as she followed the direction of everyone else's stares.

Smashed glass covered the carpet, as if a hurricane had raged through the classroom. It came from the huge windows on the far wall, which were completely shattered. Riley felt her breath catch in her throat. It was just like the break-in at the supermarket days before, when all the cat food had vanished into thin air.

But the broken window wasn't the only damage.

All across the room, the hard drives of the computers had been ripped apart, as if a huge bear had smashed the plastic covers and savaged the circuit boards inside. Everywhere Riley looked, wires and components spilled out onto the desks, like mechanical innards. She peered closer and noticed that the hard drives hadn't just been torn apart; some of the components were missing too.

'What a shame,' exclaimed Bethany Blight, a sarcastic grin on her face. 'And I was *so* looking forward to doing some coding today.'

Riley barely heard her. Her attention had shifted now, away from the computers and towards the windowsill. That was where it looked like the intruder had clambered in, leaving a trail of black slime that dripped from the ledge onto the classroom carpet.

Just like the dark liquid Riley had spotted at the crash site.

'Are you thinking what I'm thinking?'

The words came from right next to Riley, making her jerk with fright. Oli stood beside her, his eyes wide like he'd just seen a ghost. Sophia came to join them, studying the black liquid on the sill. She pulled a small notebook out of her pocket, glanced at a scrawl of notes that were scribbled there and then drew out her phone and clicked a series of photographs of the slime. Behind them, Mr Drumm had run off to get the headmaster, puffing and spluttering as if he had a cold, while Bethany and her friends complained that there wasn't a good enough signal on their phones to upload pictures of the damage onto social media.

'That gooey stuff,' Oli said, 'it isn't normal. None of this is. What's going on?'

Sophia was making some new notes in her book now, muttering to herself about slugs and drains. Riley didn't know much about Sophia, on account of the fact she was usually too busy building stuff to make many friends at school, but she did know that Sophia always seemed to know the answers in class, and if anyone could figure this out, she would probably be the one to do it.

'What do you think?' whispered Riley. 'Do you think this is connected to what happened in the forest?'

Sophia slid her notebook back into her pocket and touched the slime with the end of her pencil. She lifted it up to her nose, took a hesitant sniff and instantly looked as if she was about to throw up.

'Yes,' she replied. 'I think maybe it is.'

7

THE WATCHER

If Mo thought that things were getting weird in Shiver Point, what happened the night after the school break-in convinced him he was right.

Mo was at his bedroom window, staring at the dark mass of Howlmoor Forest, when he had the strangest feeling he wasn't alone. The sensation crept over him slowly, like goosebumps prickling his skin, a strange conviction that unseen eyes were looking in his direction from somewhere out in the darkness. On the other side of the room, his little brother Zunaid snored on obliviously, like a baby elephant.

Mo turned and stared at him for a few seconds, telling himself that the feeling he was being watched was just his imagination. For the past few days Mo had felt as if he was a detective in one of those TV shows his dad liked to watch, following a trail of clues he couldn't quite make sense of.

The strange black splodge he'd seen Sophia studying on the way to school.

The stolen cat food at the supermarket.

The mysterious break-in at school.

The pieces were there, Mo just couldn't fit them together.

He closed his eyes, trying to focus on the sounds out on the street floating in through his open bedroom window – an attempt to try and keep the room smelling vaguely fresh despite several pairs of used socks littering the floor. Mo opened his eyes again and felt a sudden stab of panic as he realised there *was* someone out there. Over on the other side of the road, partially hidden by the towering conifers, stood a tall black silhouette. At first he thought it was a dog walker, out for a late-night walk, but there was something odd about the figure, something familiar. The way it moved with jerky motions brought to mind the shape Mo had seen stalking through Howlmoor that fateful night. A glimmer of something pale flickered in the void where the creature's face should have been, a hint of a smile, grinning Mo's way.

Mo took a step backwards, fighting the urge to duck down below the windowsill and scream for his mum.

What if the person, or thing, from the woods had come looking for him? Mo wondered. What if there was someone else who wanted the meteorite and would do anything to keep it for themselves? What if they had seen Mo's face?!

In his fright, Mo caught Zunaid's piggy bank with his elbow, sending it toppling off the windowsill. He squeaked in alarm, only just managing to catch it before it hit the ground and woke the whole house up.

Mo took a deep breath, carefully relocated the piggy bank to his brother's bedside table, next to his Qur'an, and moved back to the window. Out in the darkness a dog barked, the sound echoing through the neighbourhood. Mo rubbed at his eyes, made sure there was nothing else he could manage to collide with on the windowsill, and then stared back down at the other side of the road.

Whatever he'd seen there was gone.

But Mo knew he hadn't imagined it.

There *had* been someone there, watching the house from the shadows. He was sure of it.

Mo closed the window, carefully locked it and then crouched down and made his way back to his bed. He glanced at the phone that poked out from under his pillow, then remembered that not only had the signal in Shiver Point cut out, but the only contacts he had on there were his mum, dad and Auntie Fatima. He thought for a moment, then pulled out the drawer underneath his bed and scrabbled around in there. It didn't take him long to find what he was looking for: a chunky felt-tip and a block of yellow Post-it notes that he'd used for his astronomy wall chart.

Mo chewed the lid of the felt-tip between his teeth and started to write.

After what he'd seen tonight he had to do something.

And he knew he couldn't do it on his own.

8

SAVING SHIVER POINT

Alex's mum made the best fish pie in the world. The secret to it, she always said, was to use lashings of cheese and cream, and at least three kinds of fish. Whatever the formula, it was a meal that always made Alex feel better about things, even back when they'd first moved to Shiver Point and it had seemed as if his life had come to an end.

Tonight though, as Alex dug his fork into the food on his plate and tried to force a smile, even her fish pie wasn't working. His mum was already dressed for her shift, with her hair tied back in a ponytail and her nurse's uniform on, even though she looked as if all she wanted to do was go to sleep. For most kids, the thought of being home alone with a games console and unlimited hours of screen time would sound like heaven, but Alex was starting to realise that it was nothing of the sort. It was lonely, sometimes even a little scary, especially when the old lady who was supposed to keep an eye on him could probably sleep through an earthquake.

Alex still felt a stab of anger whenever he thought about his mum's job. If not for the fact that she had been reassigned to a hospital just outside Shiver Point, he'd be back home, hanging out with his old friends.

But that wasn't what was bothering him tonight.

'How was school today?' his mum asked as she packed her own dinner into a Tupperware container to eat later.

'Yeah, it was OK, I guess,' he replied, arranging his pie into a mound in the middle of his plate. He felt his mum watching him, so he forced down another mouthful.

'Were any of your lessons affected by all the stuff that got stolen?' she asked.

'Not really. We had to move rooms period two, but apart from that today was just another boring day. Like everyone said when we moved here, nothing ever happens in Shiver Point.'

Except that wasn't quite the truth lately. No matter how much Alex would like to ignore it.

He had spotted Bethany Blight hanging out by his locker after lunch, a sly smile on her lips and a yellow Post-it note in her hand.

'What's that?' he'd asked. He knew from past experience that the best way to deal with bullies was to ignore them and walk away, but this time he couldn't help himself.

'You should know,' replied Bethany, her smile growing. 'It was on *your* locker.'

'So hand it over.'

Bethany shook her head, holding the note away. 'What's in it for me?'

'I won't tell our head of year that you've been winding people up when you're on report.'

Bethany shrugged. 'And I won't tell my brother in Year 10 to flush your head down the toilet. The note sounds important though. Something about a bunch of nerds sneaking around in a forest.'

Alex sighed. 'What do you want?'

Bethany threw a purple sketchpad in Alex's direction. 'You're good at art, even if you dress like a dweeb. So I'll tell you what – you promise to do my art homework for me and I'll give you the note. Deal?'

Alex nodded, snatching the note away from her.

'It can't be important,' continued Bethany. 'It's from *Mo*.' She started to laugh. 'Are you guys forming a gang? Geeks R Us, maybe?'

'Original,' drawled Alex.

'How about Nerds Direct?'

'Haven't you got somewhere to be?' Alex replied.

'Art homework,' called Bethany, as she walked away down the hall with a smirk. 'Don't forget! And I want to get a better grade than you!'

Once she was out of sight, Alex read the note, his mouth growing drier with every word.

Something's not right in Shiver Point. I think it's to do with what we all saw in Howlmoor Forest. Meet at Riley's. 7pm tonight. Mo.

Since that night, it felt as if whenever he closed his eyes Alex was back in Howlmoor, hearing that odd noise rip through the trees, sure that he could see something moving in the shadows. And no matter how much he tried to tell himself it was just his imagination, his brain wasn't buying it. It wasn't like he wanted to head over to Riley's to hang out with the rest of the kids that had been there, but a little voice at the back of his head nipped away at him, screaming that he needed to go along to the meeting.

'So have you got some homework to keep you busy while I'm working tonight?' his mum asked, dragging Alex back to the present.

Alex pictured the words on the Post-it and came to a sudden decision. 'Actually, I might pop out to see someone from school.'

His mum spun around from where she was packing her bag, a look of awe on her face. 'You haven't actually made a *friend* at Point Academy, have you?'

Alex shook his head. 'Don't get your hopes up. It's just a couple of kids in my class who I've been teamed up with to do a homework thing.'

'Well, hang in there. I know you miss your old friends, but surely there must be one or two kids here that are worth hanging out with.'

Alex pictured Mo and the others. 'I doubt it.'

'Just make sure you're home before it gets too dark. And call on Alison if you need anything,' his mum said as she bent to kiss his forehead before leaving for her shift.

An hour later Alex found himself heading out into the evening. It was already getting dark outside, the dying light painting the rooftops golden. He felt bad for going against what he'd told his mum, but at the same time what she didn't know wouldn't hurt her. It was only a five-minute skate to Shadow Hill cemetery, and it wasn't long before he saw the graveyard in the distance, the small cottage Riley lived in just across the road from it.

Up close it was a little creepier than he remembered. The small wooden gate opened onto a gravel path, which led up to a chocolate-box cottage, wooden beams and trailing ivy making it look like something from a fairy tale. The place seemed deserted, except for a stooped old guy with a grey Afro and a walking stick who was limping around the garden, watering flowers. Now that he was standing by the gate, Alex wasn't sure why he'd come, and he was even less sure he wanted to stay.

'Hey! Up here!'

The words made Alex jerk in fright, and he looked up to see a rope ladder tumbling down towards him from a huge oak tree that stood next to the fence. A familiar face hovered at the top of the ladder.

'We weren't sure you'd come,' called Riley.

Alex stared at her, unsure how to respond. 'I'm still not sure why I did.'

Riley studied him for a moment. Her outfit was as eccentric as usual: a bright metallic T-shirt covered by a pair of dungarees embroidered with a fluffy dayglo unicorn.

'Well, I'm glad you did. Everyone else is already here, so come on up.'

Alex gripped hold of the first rung and started to pull himself past the branches. Now that he knew where to look, he couldn't believe he hadn't seen the huge treehouse, right in the centre of the oak, pieced together from dozens of different types of timber. He reached the top of the ladder, grabbed hold of a handle to pull himself up, and peered inside.

It was Alex's first real treehouse, and he was pleasantly surprised. A huddle of beanbags was slouched on the wooden floorboards, and it felt pretty cosy. A bench ran along one side, littered with wires and tools and bits of everything from games consoles to dismantled toasters, a handful of weird-looking inventions rearing up from among the mass of parts. The darkness was brightened by several lava lamps, bubbling away silently in the corners, and a host of fairy lights glittered up in the rafters.

'Wow,' Alex heard himself mumble. 'This place is something else.'

A shy smile flashed on Riley's face as she retreated over to the bench, taking a seat next to the pile of wires and circuit boards. 'Thanks, it's my den.'

As Alex stepped inside, he noticed a quartet of faces looking in his direction, like a Howlmoor Forest reunion.

'So why did you guys invite me here?' Alex asked. 'If you're going to play *Dungeons and Dragons*, I'm leaving right now.'

Mo was perched against the far wall, as far away from the open doorway and the long drop down as was humanly possible. He glanced up at Alex's words, a hopeful look on his face. 'Has . . . has someone got a D&D set? If I'd known, I'd have brought my level-five Dwarf Berserker!'

Sophia sat a few feet away, brushing a cobweb off the elbow of her school uniform. 'He's being sarcastic, Mo,' she sighed, pulling that all-too-familiar notebook out of her pocket. 'And you're the one that summoned us all here. You told me that you chose the treehouse because there's no parents around, and because you want to keep all this secret, so you know better than anyone that we've got far more important things to do than roll odd-shaped dice around and fight imaginary orcs.'

Oli was slouched in a beanbag in the corner, dwarfed by a huge *Call of Duty* hoodie, his scruffy Nikes poking out from a pair of even messier tracksuit bottoms. He had a strange look on his face. Alex thought it was a look he'd never really seen on the boy before, despite all the times he'd seen Oli get chewed out by the teachers at Point Academy.

If he didn't know better, Alex would say Oli was *nervous*.

'Why are we here?' Mo asked, taking a deep breath as if he was trying to summon up the courage for what he was about to say. 'I guess we're here to try to save Shiver Point.'

9

COUNT ME OUT

'Save Shiver Point from what?' asked Alex, rolling his eyes even though he felt a nervous sweat break out on his forehead. 'That little notebook that Sophia carries everywhere with her?'

Riley leaned forward from where she was sitting by the workbench. 'Mo's right. Something's going on in Shiver Point. There's been too many weird things happening since that lump of rock came down in the forest.'

'Like what?' demanded Alex, not sure where the conversation was going. After what had happened in the woods, he'd made a deliberate point of avoiding the others, and once again he wondered why he'd come here tonight.

Was it because really, deep down, he knew things weren't quite right?

'Slugs, for starters,' shot back Sophia, a spiky look on her face.

'*Slugs?*' Alex repeated. 'What are you talking about?'

Sophia looked at him like a teacher that was beginning to run out of patience. 'I'm talking about big black slugs, all around town. Except they aren't slugs at all. They're black, and shiny, but they've also got three eyes and are far bigger than any slug I've ever seen before. They also smell, like, really bad. I've seen three of them now, and there's nothing like them in any of the reference books I've checked.'

'So let me get this right – we're going to save Shiver Point from . . . slugs.'

Mo held up his hand, like a nervous kid at the back of the class. 'It isn't just the slugs. It's all the other stuff too. The break-ins at the supermarket and school. And . . . and . . .'

'Go on,' urged Riley. 'Tell him.'

A frightened look slid over Mo's face, and he seemed to shrink under his black beanie. 'I saw something from my bedroom window last night. A figure, on the other side of the street. I thought I was dreaming it, but then this morning I found a footprint in my neighbour's garden.'

He took a deep breath.

'A black, slimy one.'

'Black slimy footprints,' repeated Alex, unable to keep the mocking tone from his voice. '*Right*.'

For a moment nobody spoke. Oli shifted on his beanbag, staring at Mo like he'd seen a ghost. Alex was surprised Oli was even there. He seemed the kind of kid who spent most of his time running wild, not hanging around with rule-followers like Mo, Sophia and Riley. So what Oli said next shocked Alex even more . . .

'I believe you, Mo,' he murmured. 'There's this weird feeling around town, like something bad's coming. Not to mention that smell, hanging in the air like everyone's been eating sprouts for weeks on end.'

'Let me get this straight,' Alex said, scratching his head in confusion. 'You asked me to come here for *this*? Because you've got a *feeling*? Because you've seen a few *slugs* and the drains are playing up?'

Riley's eyes were locked on Alex like she couldn't quite figure him out.

'You were there that night in the forest. You saw what we saw. And if you didn't have suspicions already, why did you come here tonight?' she asked.

Alex didn't have an answer for that question. That little voice was suddenly back in his head, telling him that he needed to listen, the one that had chattered away to him when he'd been lost in Howlmoor Forest.

'I've seen a lot of horror films,' announced Oli, starting to look more confident. 'My sister loves those ancient movies from back before mobile phones, like *The Thing*, *Alien*, *Predator*, *War of the Worlds*. And all the stuff that happens in those films, it feels like *this*.'

'Next you'll be telling me you saw this on an episode of *Doctor Who*!' said Alex, exasperation creeping into his voice. 'If things are so bad, why aren't the grown-ups doing something?'

'They are,' answered Sophia. 'The mayor's called a town meeting this weekend . We haven't had one of those for years.'

She opened the pristine backpack that she carried around school, sorting through her neatly organised schoolbooks and folders until she located what she wanted.

'Look,' she said, holding up a newspaper cutting for the rest of the group to see.

THE SHIVERING POST

Mayor calls emergency Shiver Point meeting!

Reported by Damian Thorn

Last night, Mayor David Drake called an emergency meeting to discuss the concerning events of the past two weeks. With a string of mysterious break-ins and unexplained thefts, not to mention the loss of the internet and phone signal, Shiver Point's residents are up in arms.

'We can't go on like this,' complained local supermarket manager Andy Clifford. 'It feels like the whole town is falling apart.

First it was my store that got broken into, then the school. People are saying that it's just a prank, and that all the burglars took was some cat food, but it's much more serious than that. Three pallets' worth of cat food went missing overnight, and no one has any idea how. I mean, you'd need a forklift truck to lift that much food! How did they even get it out of the store? It doesn't make sense. I don't feel safe locking up at night any more, and what are people supposed to feed their cats? Tuna?!'

Mrs Esme Cawley, headteacher of Point Academy, said: 'I can confirm that there was a break-in at the school, and that the ICT facilities were targeted. Police are currently trying to trace the culprits, but that doesn't help the disruption to lessons. The baffling thing is, dozens of computers were damaged, but the only parts taken were the network interface controllers, the component that allows the computers to connect to the internet. They're not even worth much money.'

Sunday night will mark the first Shiver Point town meeting in three years. The last time a meeting was called was in response to a string of suspicious vegetable disappearances from allotments across town. While the pumpkin and marrow thefts were eventually traced to a herd of rogue ponies that had escaped from a local stables, it remains to be seen who is responsible for the break-ins and loss of communications, and how the mayor plans to deal with it. Representatives from the *Shivering Post* contacted the mayor's office, but he is unavailable for comment at this time. We'll keep you up to date with this breaking story as it develops.

Alex finished reading the article. 'So what's your theory? That Shiver Point is being attacked by an army of giant stinky space slugs that can break into schools and supermarkets and chew through the internet cables?'

A noise echoed outside, an owl hooting in the dusk, and everyone jumped at the sound. Riley took a look out of the window and then rolled up the treehouse ladder, clipping it into place by the entrance. Mo shuffled closer to the others, as if he didn't want his words to carry beyond their circle.

'You were all there that first night. Those rocks we found were strange. Everything about that night was strange. And things in Shiver Point have been strange ever since. Maybe someone else was there with us in the forest. Maybe they're up to something and they're trying to scare us.'

Alex felt a trickle of unease at the words. He didn't want to admit it, but he still couldn't shake the feeling that he'd seen a figure in the woods that night too.

'So now we're saying that it's a zookeeper with his giant slug pets that he can somehow control?' he said, trying to keep the jitter from his voice.

'You know we're right,' insisted Riley, directing her words at Alex. 'I can see it on your face.'

'Something's going to happen, and when it does, the fact that the internet and phones are down means no one will be able to call for help,' said Oli. 'Just like in all the scariest horror films.'

Alex stayed quiet for a moment, replaying in his mind the evidence the others had laid out before him. He didn't want to believe a word of it, but all the same . . .

Sophia jabbed the chewed end of her pen at Alex. 'So are you with us? We're in this together. We *need* you.' She paused, as if she wasn't quite willing to admit that, for once, there was a problem she couldn't solve by herself. 'Maybe right now we can't see how all this is connected, but we will, if we keep investigating.'

Somehow the thought of being part of this group was even more disturbing than the weird goings-on since that night with the light in the sky. Alex had had friends back home, and he'd lost them when he moved. The last thing he wanted was to get a new group of friends, only to lose them if his mum got moved on again. He felt that familiar surge of anger, the one he experienced whenever he thought about how good life had been before they'd had to move to Shiver Point.

'This is ridiculous!' he blurted before he could stop himself. 'Can you hear yourselves? Stinking slugs? Black slime? If you guys want to get all Scooby-Doo and run around chasing shadows, that's up to you, but count me out!'

He didn't wait for a reply. Before anyone could say a word, he stomped over to the exit, unclipped the hook so that the rope ladder tumbled down towards the ground, and scrambled down the ladder.

10

HOME ALONE

A noise woke Alex up.

The sound of something pushing through the trees at the bottom of the garden cut through his sleep. It was followed by odd, shuffling footsteps on the path that led up to the back door.

Alex pushed off the covers, sat up and told himself it was just his imagination. It was the middle of the night and he'd been on edge since the meeting in the treehouse earlier that evening, the evidence that the others had laid out chipping away at his insistence that things were fine. On the way home Alex had ignored the smell in the air, refused to look anywhere near the forest or at any drains, and done all he could to convince himself that life in the town was as boring as ever.

But things had taken a turn for the worse when Alex had arrived home. He'd walked up his path and seen Alison taking out her recycling ready for collection day tomorrow. There was nothing unusual about that, of course, even though the box looked fairly heavy for a little old lady. But what *was* unusual was the contents of her recycling.

Alex had felt his breath catch in his throat, his feet scraping to a sudden halt as he stared into the box to make sure he wasn't seeing things.

It was full of small, empty cans.

Empty cans that had once contained cat food.

Alex had swallowed drily, wondering if he should ask his neighbour what she was doing. Alison had no pets, not even a goldfish, so how she'd got through so many tins of cat food was a mystery.

Alison had dumped the box at the bottom of the drive with a loud crash. When she'd noticed Alex watching her, she'd smiled, a cold, vacant grin, cuffed at her runny nose and then made her way back towards her house. And maybe it had been Alex's imagination, but whatever Alison had wiped from her nose, whatever she'd transferred onto the sleeve of her pale blue jumper looked . . . kind of black.

Just like slime.

Alex had sprinted for his front door, slammed it shut behind him and gone up to his room, where he shoved his desk in front of his door. Alison had a cold, he told himself as he paced his bedroom, that's all it was. And maybe she was looking after a cat for a friend, despite the fact that she seemed to dislike animals – in fact, she had a habit of scuttling outside with a broom if a neighbour's cat so much as set a paw on her lawn or went near her flower beds. The thoughts had bounced around Alex's head like a pinball, jerking him awake whenever he started to drift off until he eventually fell into a deep, dreamless sleep.

But now something had woken him up. And he wasn't sure he wanted to know what.

Alex lay frozen, straining his ears for any more sounds coming from the garden.

There!

The noise of someone twisting the handle on the back door downstairs.

'Mum,' he croaked warily. 'Mum, is that you?'

Nothing.

Alex peered at the phone on his bedside table. It was almost 1 a.m. Sometimes his mum got kept late at work, and didn't come back until almost dawn. He could go downstairs, sneak out the front way and knock on Alison's door, but after what he'd seen earlier, that was almost as scary a proposition as staying put.

Alex flinched as he heard it again: the sound of the handle being tested, followed by the rattle of the door in its frame. If it *had* been Alex's mum, by now she would have slid her key into the lock and stepped into the hallway. She also would have come in the front door, like a normal person.

Which meant that someone else was trying to get inside the house.

Trying to ignore his fear, Alex shuffled across the room, doing his best to navigate his way in the darkness. He bit back a scream as his foot came down on something sharp. Wincing, Alex limped onwards, glancing down to see Lego

Thor lying where he'd just stepped, one arm sheared off, the hammer fallen from its grasp. Ignoring the throbbing in his foot, Alex made it to the window and tried to get a glimpse outside without being seen.

What he saw set his heart thundering in his chest.

There was someone down by the back door, a dark indistinct figure. Maybe it was a trick of the light, but it seemed as if the edges of the figure were shifting, moving, like interference on a television screen. There was something else too: a scattering of small black shapes squirming around on the patio nearby.

A wave of unreality washed over Alex as his brain made sense of what he was seeing.

Slugs.

The things down by the back door looked like *slugs*.

Alex edged away from the window, trying to stop the panic that was threatening to engulf him. Whoever was out there, *what*ever was out there, it couldn't get inside, could it?

A moment later Alex heard it – an odd wet sound, like when his gran made the gravy too thick and it squished out from the jug in gooey lumps.

Alex didn't have time to try to figure out what the noise was, because it was immediately followed by the sound of footsteps on the kitchen floorboards, then the creak of the hallway door.

'Mum?' Alex hissed again, tears biting at his eyes. Except he already knew that whoever had just come inside definitely wasn't his mum.

Maybe it isn't even human, whispered a voice at the back of Alex's head, chilling him to the bone. He thought of that meteor flaming through the sky, and all the horror movies Oli had mentioned. They all had one thing in common. He snatched at his phone, pressed dial on his mum's number and was confronted with the 'no signal' notification.

Alex's fear gave way to all-out panic.

He glanced around the room, searching for somewhere to hide. His closet was too small, under the bed too obvious, behind the door too easy to spot.

He was doomed.

More sounds drifted up the stairs. Slow, shuffling footsteps that were too heavy to belong to Alex's mum, or a human at all if Alex was being totally honest, and occasional gasping breaths, like someone with a really bad chest infection.

Alex's panic turned to full-blown terror. He scrambled across to his bedroom window again, this time sliding open the latch and peering outside. It was a long drop to the ground, onto solid concrete, but he didn't have a choice. He couldn't stay here! With the sound of the intruder's footsteps coming closer, Alex climbed up onto the sill, leaned out to his left and spotted the drainpipe. Maybe if he could just make it those few inches, he could shimmy up the pipe and he might be able to haul himself onto the roof.

It was the only chance he had.

Alex stretched out, trying to keep his weight centred, one hand firmly on the edge of the window while groping for the drainpipe with the other. He felt his fingers brush the metal, but it was *just* out of reach.

He was going to have to jump.

And pray the pipe held his weight.

Alex had no time to think the decision through, or to wonder how many bones he might break if the drainpipe sheared off the wall and sent him down to the ground. Instead, he gritted his teeth and went for it, letting go of the window frame and leaping through the air.

A moment of weightlessness later, his fingers grasped the pipe. He wrapped himself around it like a koala bear, caught his breath and then started to climb. As he hauled himself up onto the roof he heard his bedroom door swing open, the desk that had been holding it closed smashing to the floor.

Making himself as small as he could, Alex curled up into a ball on the roof, just above his bedroom window. He wasn't safe yet. If whatever was inside the house had heard him, if it realised where he'd gone, there was nowhere left to run. Alex clamped his jaws together, trying to silence the chattering of his teeth in case it gave him away.

In the darkness, the wait seemed endless. Alex couldn't see inside his bedroom from where he hid, but he knew the intruder was there. Through half-closed eyelids he peered towards the edge of the roof, half expecting a set of clawed fingertips to appear, or an awful, twisted face.

What Alex did see was almost worse.

A fat, bloated slug slithered up the drainpipe, three spindly antennae trembling as if tasting the air.

It took several seconds for Alex to realise what it was doing.

Searching for him.

Alex watched as the slug slid up onto the roof, leaving a wet, black trail behind it, like dark snot. Any second now it would notice him. And what if it had some way to alert whatever was in his bedroom below?

Alex knew there was only one thing for it.

As quietly as he could, he reached out, shoving the creature with his big toe so that it tumbled off the roof. As his skin brushed the slug's slimy body, Alex felt a wave of revulsion. He wished he was wearing socks.

An instant later he heard a sharp plop, like a water balloon bursting as it hit the ground. He pictured the slug splatting on impact with the patio, and felt like he might be sick.

Pulling back his foot, Alex wrapped his arms around himself and waited. Time dragged on, seconds turning to minutes, minutes crawling to hours, the blackness of night gradually giving way to the grey light of dawn.

Alex didn't move from his hiding place until the first glimmer of sunlight flickered on the horizon. And he didn't dare look over the roof's edge again.

11

SECOND CHANCES

Riley was tinkering with a circuit board in her den when she saw the figure drift into sight on her homemade CCTV. She dropped her screwdriver, edged closer to the screen and felt her breath catch in her throat.

She recognised the boy on her screen, but he looked a lot more scared than the last time she'd seen him.

Alex had his skateboard tucked under one arm, the same slouchy hoodie he'd been wearing yesterday hanging down to his knees, and his hair was even messier than usual. He looked as if he'd slept in his clothes and run through a hundred nightmares.

Riley abandoned her tinkering, ran over to the treehouse door and let down the ladder. It was early, but she liked sleeping in the den, curling up in her sleeping bag above the town, right until the grass started to get frosty. Her grandad never minded – he'd helped her build the treehouse after all, the summer before his arthritis got too bad.

'You look like you've seen a ghost,' she called down.

Alex lifted his head to look at her. His eyes were red-rimmed, his face pale.

'Worse,' he shouted back, a tremble in his voice.

'What do you want?' she asked, remembering the way he'd stormed out the night before.

'I just want to talk.'

The look on Alex's face confirmed something bad had happened overnight. Despite the fact that he always seemed so aloof at school, Riley couldn't help feel a weird kind of kinship with him, and the way he didn't seem to quite fit in either. She climbed down the rope ladder and gestured towards the cemetery that sat across from her house.

'I thought you were too cool to hang out with us,' she grumbled as she hauled herself up onto the cemetery wall and sat down.

Alex stared at her for a moment, then clambered up alongside her. 'No. I just wasn't interested in making new friends.'

Riley nodded, watching the morning light glint on the old stone of the gravestones. Some people found the graveyard creepy, but not Riley. Living across from the cemetery, she felt like the crumbling monuments and gravestones and the chapel at the top of the hill were the only neighbours she had.

'That makes two of us. I don't really have any friends either.'

'I have friends,' Alex said defensively. But then he sighed. 'They're all just back home. Where I used to live. I didn't think it was worth trying to make any new friends in Shiver Point when I was so sure one day we'd be able to go back home. That's why I was in the forest that night. I thought I could find a meteorite and sell it so my mum could quit her job here and we could move back. But after last night, I just want to forget I ever saw that light in the sky . . .'

Tears shone in his eyes and he swiped at his face with the sleeve of his hoodie.

'What's up?' she asked.

Alex took a deep breath and then he launched into the story of his late-night visitor. Riley felt her blood run cold as he recounted the events, especially the fact that he'd stayed hidden up on the roof until dawn.

'All of this . . .' she asked in a shaky voice once he'd finished, 'it really happened?'

Alex gave her a heavy nod. 'You think I'd make up something like this?'

A police car slid past, the officer behind the wheel giving the two kids on the wall a long, cold, menacing stare before cruising off.

'No. I guess not. So where was your mum all this time?'

'She works nights at the hospital, the one just outside town. She got back around seven this morning, but there was no way I could tell her what had happened. I'm pretty sure the only people who might believe me were the ones who were there in the forest that night.'

Riley fired him a salty look. 'The ones you said were making things up?'

Alex leaned back, closing his eyes. 'I'm sorry, OK? I was wrong, but I just . . . I was freaked out.'

He fell silent and Riley found herself going over his story again, taking it apart.

'OK, apology accepted. So this thing you saw, this figure, what did it look like?'

Alex shivered at the question. 'I didn't see its face. I caught a glimpse of it by the back door, and it looked kind of . . . slimy. All I really saw clearly was the slugs. They were bad enough.'

The wind whipped across the graveyard, sending a flurry of brown leaves dancing towards the ground.

'What do you think it was doing there?'

Alex opened his eyes, a frightened look shining there. 'That was pretty much all I thought about while I was sitting there last night on the roof. Was it after my mum? Was it after me? Was it because we saw it in the forest that night and it wanted to make sure I wouldn't tell anyone?'

'Did it leave anything behind? Anything we could use to prove what happened?'

Alex shook his head, staring at the cemetery chapel's bell tower that overlooked the town. 'There was some weird black gunk on the door handles, a little more on the carpet on the stairs. But the door was locked, and the windows weren't broken like at the supermarket or at school, so I still can't figure out how it got in. I cleaned up what I could before my mum got home. She's got enough to worry about without me freaking her out with all this.'

He took a deep breath, staring up at the sky where a plane painted a white trail of vapour against the blue. 'I knew you and Mo and the others were right. I just didn't want to admit it. But . . . that night in the forest, that rock that came from the stars . . . something else came down with it, didn't it? Something like . . . like an alien?'

Riley stared at him for a moment, putting herself back in Howlmoor, that odd sound shrieking through the trees. 'Yeah. I think maybe it did. But why is it here? What does it want with Shiver Point?'

Alex had no response, his face haunted.

Riley scrabbled around in her back pocket, pulling out a big plastic block, like the mobile phones people used to use back in the Dark Ages.

'What is that?' asked Alex.

Riley looked suddenly self-conscious. 'It's a two-way radio,' she explained. 'Like a walkie-talkie but a bit more powerful. I bought an old set from the charity shop, had a play with them and boosted them so I could keep in touch with my grandad, or my friends, if . . . if I ever made any. It transmits and receives on a single frequency wireless signal, so it works even in places where a mobile phone has no reception.'

Alex didn't really understand, but he nodded as if he did and watched as Riley clicked a button, causing the radio to hiss into life.

'When you left, the others soon did too,' she told Alex. 'It was like you leaving made it all fall apart. But I made each of them take a walkie-talkie, just in case things got worse. I think I've got an idea what we need to do next, but we can't do it on our own.'

She twisted a dial, held down a red button and spoke into the speaker.

'Hey guys, it's Riley. Can you hear me? If you can, Alex is here. That thing from the woods broke into his house last night. It sounds weird, but the slugs were there too. It was pretty scary. We need to find out what's going on, before it's too late. I think we need to head into Howlmoor. Meet us by the old gate on the forest road at seven thirty.'

12

IF YOU GO INTO THE WOODS TODAY . . .

It didn't seem possible, but with Alex's story running through his head, Mo thought Howlmoor Forest felt even more creepy than the first time.

'Whose idea was it to come here at night?' he muttered, checking the batteries on his torch for the thousandth time while the rest of the group stood at the edge of the woodland, trying to summon the courage to venture in.

'Sorry.' Alex shot Mo an apologetic look. 'It was my fault. I had to stay at home all day while my mum slept, and make sure she'd safely left for work this evening before I set off. After last night, after that . . . thing got in, I couldn't risk leaving her on her own in the house.'

He sighed, pulling out his phone as if to check there hadn't been some kind of distress call from her. Riley stood alongside them, the goggles she'd had that first night in the forest back on her head. She placed a reassuring hand on Mo's shoulder, making him jump in fright.

'Tomorrow's Sunday, so even if it takes us all night to explore the forest we can sleep it off.'

'I wasn't too worried about . . . Wait, *all night*?' stuttered Mo, his hopes of being home in an hour lying in tatters on the forest floor. 'What are we going to be doing here that takes *all night*?' He might have been keen to find out what was stalking the town, but not so desperate that he was willing to stay in the forest until dawn.

Sophia turned around, the LED head torch she was wearing momentarily blinding Mo. She looked as if she was about to embark on an SAS training course, with a utility vest over her school uniform, a pair of hiking boots on her feet and a huge backpack slung over her shoulders.

'What have you got in there?' asked Oli, gesturing at the bag. 'Your homework, in case you get bored?'

Sophia shot him a withering look. 'Maybe you should spend a little more time concentrating rather than trying to be funny. And to answer your question, Mo, we're here to find where it all started, to examine those rocks and to search for clues. You were the one who started to put things together, so you should be all for this.' Mo appreciated the effort Sophia was making to be encouraging, but he grimaced nevertheless. 'Maybe we can find some more evidence tonight, and prove to the adults that something's going on and that Shiver Point's in danger,' Sophia continued.

'Or maybe the person – or thing – that came after Alex last night will find us,' suggested Mo. 'I've been looking forward to half-term for the past eight weeks. Now that it's finally here, what if I don't live to enjoy it?'

'There's five of us, and only one of that freak,' reassured Oli, reaching into his jacket and drawing out a plastic super soaker that he had hidden away. 'And if we do run into trouble, I'll take care of it with this.'

He spun the gun on his index finger, trying to dazzle the others with his skills but only managing to release the plug so that freezing water soaked his jeans.

'Oops,' he moaned, rubbing at his legs with the sleeve of his jacket. 'I haven't got that move quite right yet.'

'Somehow I'm not sure how useful that's going to be,' said Alex, turning away to hide his smile and starting to push through the undergrowth.

'Before we go any further, we'd better check we've got everything we need,' Sophia instructed, pointing the head-torch beam down onto her ever-present notebook. 'Drinks. Snacks. Phones. And –'

'What's the use of phones?' interrupted Oli, his super soaker now safely stashed back in his jacket. 'We can't get a signal in Howlmoor, can we?'

'We can hardly get a signal anywhere in Shiver Point, but phones have cameras, and that could be useful,' Sophia explained, fiddling with the settings on her torch.

'Good idea – get a few Howlmoor selfies to remember tonight by?' taunted Oli, putting on a posh voice that was supposed to mimic Sophia's. 'Look, everyone, here's me and the slug whisperer, out for an evening stroll.'

Sophia turned to face Oli, the bright beam of her head torch making him wince. 'In my experience, there's usually a rational explanation for everything. I know weird things have been happening in Shiver Point, and you all know I love a mystery, but until I get photographic evidence I'm not going to start believing in aliens.'

The word *aliens* made Mo want to turn and run. He didn't know when they'd all agreed that was what they were facing, but right now it seemed the most likely explanation. He glanced down at his wrist, pressing the little button at the side of his Minecraft watch so that the blocky face lit up. It was almost 8 p.m., and they hadn't even properly got started yet. He looked up at the thick black clouds that were stopping the moon from breaking through, and hoped that his little brother wouldn't wake up in their shared room and raise the alarm that he was missing.

'I almost broke my neck climbing out of my window without switching the light on. How did you guys manage to get out without being seen?' he asked. Maybe he could learn a thing or two about sneaking out, seeing as he'd never done it before, and the rest of them seemed pretty practised at it.

'My mum works nights,' explained Alex, pulling his hood up as a fine layer of drizzle started to fall. 'And right now I hope she stays there.'

Riley looked up at the sky, wiping the screen of her goggles dry. 'My grandad goes to bed really early, and besides, he knows I sleep out in the treehouse until the nights get colder.'

'I'm so well behaved that neither of my mums would dream of me doing something like this,' Sophia said. 'I left the bedside light on and built a line of pillows on my bed just in case though. They'll never even know I'm gone.' She looked pretty happy with her ingenuity.

Oli laughed to himself, glancing back in the direction of Shiver Point. 'There's a lot of bad things about being the middle child, but there's the odd good one too. Between my big sisters and their music and my little sister and her tantrums, Mum and Dad generally leave me in peace. When my luck's in, I get to lock my bedroom door, turn out the lights and play Xbox until it's nearly morning.'

'How do you get up for school?' asked Mo.

Oli picked at a piece of what looked like dried peanut butter stuck to the side of his mouth. 'I don't. That's why I have so many detentions. If it wasn't for my Xbox, I wouldn't even be here.'

'No offence, but *why* are you here?' asked Alex. 'I mean, I kind of get it with the others. Sophia can't get enough of school and lessons, and I guess Riley and Mo are kind of the same, but you . . . I mean, don't take this the wrong way, but you seem to spend most of your time at school sitting outside the headmaster's office rather than actually learning.'

Oli stared at him for a few seconds then shrugged. 'I spend all my time at home shooting aliens on my controller. I guess I just wanted to know if they're real or not. And I spend all my time at school doing the wrong thing. I don't mean to, it just kind of . . . happens. So I guess that, just for once, I wanted to do the right thing.'

Sophia gave Oli a curious look, like she'd never really noticed him before. When he began to squirm under her gaze, she switched back to her usual no-nonsense self. 'Well, as nice as it is for us all to get to know each other better, we haven't come here to spend all night socialising, have we? We need to get started, or we're going to run out of time. Any more questions?'

Oli smirked. 'I have one. Why do you always wear your school unform? I mean, haven't you got any normal clothes?'

It was all Mo could do to hold in a snort of laughter. He'd been wondering the same thing.

Sophia straightened her blazer self-consciously, polishing the prefect badge on her lapel. 'Of course I have other clothes. I just . . . I just like my uniform. Wearing it reminds me of what I'm good at. Organising people, and . . . studying. Now let's go.'

In the darkness, it was hard to work out exactly where the meteorite had come down. Everywhere Mo shone his torch looked the same, an infinity of trees casting ugly, menacing shadows. The last time he'd been here, the light from the thing that had fallen from the sky had drawn them all towards it, or at least Mo thought it had. A little part of his brain still clung to the hope that the whole thing had been their imagination, and the spot where they'd found the rocks would look empty and normal this time.

As usual, he ended up being disappointed.

'Maybe we should go back,' he said to no one in particular. 'Maybe we should forget the whole thing and just –'

'Over there!' exclaimed Sophia, an edge of excitement to her voice. 'It's there!'

Their little group followed her torch beam, converging on the now-familiar clearing in the trees.

The rocks weren't glowing any more, Mo quickly realised, but they were still there, scattered across the scorched grass. Maybe it was because Howlmoor was so sprawling, but it looked as if no one had been there in the two weeks since that night. It felt colder here too, as if the sun never made it this deep into the forest.

Before anyone could stop him, Oli took a step forward, picked up a piece of rock and held it in the light from Alex's torch. 'I guess we didn't dream it after all,' he said, as if he'd read Mo's mind. 'So what do we do now?'

Riley pointed down towards the patches of black liquid on the grass, also there just as Mo had remembered them.

'It's just like the slime in the computer room,' Riley observed, studying the splodges with her night goggles.

'And the goo in my hallway,' echoed Alex, the colour draining from his face.

'You know,' Mo murmured, more to himself than to any of the others, 'they look like footprints to me.'

'Whatever they are, they lead off into those trees,' Sophia announced, a determined shine in her eyes. 'And we need to follow them. Oli, Alex, come with me. Mo, Riley, you stay here and see what you can find.'

Mo experienced a jolt of terror. 'No, no way! There's no way we're splitting up! Haven't you heard about what happens to the people who split up in all those horror films Oli loves? If we split up, we'll never make it out of these woods!'

Alex nodded, gesturing towards the black footprints. 'He's right. If we're going to do this, we need to stick together. Come on, let's all go – there's nothing else this crash site can tell us. I think the answers lie deeper in the forest.'

He looked scared, and who could blame him after what he'd been through the night before, but Mo watched him set off into the trees nonetheless. There was definitely more to Alex than met the eye; one moment he didn't want anything to do with the whole business, the next he was the one leading them all further into the forest.

Mo took a deep breath, steeled himself and set off after the others. He couldn't get rid of the sinking feeling that this was a *very* bad idea.

13

CALL THE POLICE!

If it felt like they'd been walking for hours, Oli realised the reason was because they had. He scowled down at his watch, stifled a yawn and continued to trudge along behind the others.

They'd lost sight of the trail of weird black footprints ages ago, and it felt to Oli as if they were just wandering around, lost, not even sure what they were looking for. He was getting bored, and things didn't go well when he was bored. Boredom was usually the thing that got him in trouble. It made his mind drift at school, so that he stole the pencil case from the kid next to him, or started tapping his pen on the desk, or said the wrong thing to the teacher.

Boredom was Oli's arch-enemy. And right now Oli was so bored that he actually wouldn't mind meeting an alien.

At least it would be more exciting than this.

They'd found a few things in the forest, but nothing that he'd class as exciting. There'd been a battered old shack, like something from a fairy tale, sitting tucked among the trees. Sophia had shone her torch inside, but it looked as if the place had been abandoned years ago. After that they'd stumbled across a murky swamp, the kind of place that in the films Oli had watched would have zombies lurking under the surface, but the only thing poking out was an old rusty bicycle.

'It's going to be light soon,' complained Mo, for what felt to Oli like the thousandth time. 'And the good news is we haven't been eaten yet. Maybe it's time we left. Quit while we're ahead and all that.'

They were just crossing a rickety wooden bridge that spanned Misty Creek, the fast-running river that cut through Howlmoor and ran all the way to the sea. Riley paused, one hand on the bridge's railing, and pointed towards the far bank.

'There's something over that way. Some kind of wall, I think, where the forest comes to an end. Let's make that our final check and then call it a day.'

They trudged the last few metres through the trees, the beams from their torches probing the way ahead like helicopter spotlights. As the trees thinned out and the forest fell away, Oli realised that they'd arrived at a boring wall of jagged stone, its face covered in moss and vines and trickles of running water. He was starting to wish he'd stayed at home and played on his Xbox after all, even if going online wasn't an option right now.

'Hey, what's that?' called Alex, shining his torch towards the bottom of the rock face. Oli squinted, noticing something glinting in the beam of light.

The five of them made their way towards the shimmer. As they got closer, Oli saw that it was a metal grille, a large circular gate set into the wall of rock. Alex shone his torch through the bars, illuminating a long thin tunnel that disappeared into the distance.

'Where do you think it . . .'

Alex's words died in his throat as the sound of footsteps drifted out of the darkness.

Oli peered closer, just making out a tall thin figure heading along the tunnel towards them.

'Someone's coming!' hissed Mo. 'We need to hide, quick!'

They scrambled back towards the trees, keeping low like a group of soldiers caught behind enemy lines. Oli had wanted a little excitement, but someone coming out of a cave like that Gollum guy in *The Hobbit* was taking things a bit too far. Everyone dived behind tree trunks, flicking their torches off. A whimper escaped Mo's lips as the darkness closed in, but it wasn't as black as it had been deeper in the woods. There was a hint of grey to the sky now, Oli reckoned, a glimmer of light at the edge of the trees.

'Nearly dawn,' whispered Sophia, jabbing a finger up towards the sky.

Everyone jumped as the creak of the gate reached them through the trees. Mo started to shuffle backwards, but Alex reached out, grabbing onto his arm. Riley lay on her tummy, studying the figure through those clever goggles of hers.

'It's a man,' she narrated, peering towards the gate. 'He . . . he's got something in his hand, a can of drink or something. He looks ordinary enough, except he's wearing a uniform. In fact, I think he might be . . . I think it might be a *policeman.*'

Mo's eyes lit up in relief. 'Then we're safe! Maybe we could tell him why we're here, what we've seen!'

Sophia held up her hand, a patrol leader stopping one of her group from rushing headlong into danger. 'Let's just wait a moment and see what he does. If it looks like –'

A dull, rhythmic beeping made them all jump. Riley swore, grabbing the goggles from her head. 'My night goggles – they're running low on battery!'

She clicked a button on the goggles, silencing the noise, but it was already too late. Over by the tunnel's entrance, the policeman's head snapped up and he pulled out his own torch, shining it towards Oli and the others.

'Who's there?' he called, coming a step closer. 'Come out, right now!'

Mo was the first to break, stumbling out into the light, his hands raised. Sophia followed with a sigh, knowing the game was up, and the others followed until it was just Oli left behind his tree trunk. He was tempted to stay, but Mo beckoned him out, ruining any chance he had of keeping hidden.

The police officer tossed the can he was drinking from to one side with a metallic clank and slid his torch beam from one face to the next.

'What are you all doing here?' he asked. Despite the fact he'd just come out of a secret tunnel in the woods, his uniform was neat and pressed, his face pale and clean shaven.

'We're . . .' started Alex, looking at the others for help.

'Geocaching,' finished Oli, nodding in satisfaction at his own answer.

'You're *what*?' asked the officer, his words dripping with suspicion.

'You know,' continued Oli, '*geocaching*. That super nerdy hobby where you search for

Tupperware containers and then swap the rubbish you find for something even more useless.' He jabbed a finger at Mo. 'It was *his* idea.'

While Mo protested his innocence as if he'd been accused of stealing a Porsche, Sophia cleared her throat pointedly, signalling with her foot towards the can at the officer's feet. Second by second, it was growing lighter in the forest, the weak glow of the rising sun penetrating the trees. Oli stared down at the policeman's boots, wondering what it was that Sophia was trying to tell them.

And then it suddenly clicked. The man hadn't been drinking from a can.

He'd been eating.

Eating *cat food*.

Mo started to give out a high-pitched whine as he figured it out too. He sounded like the kettle that Oli's gran stuck on the stove when she needed a cup of tea.

'Didn't that . . . didn't a load of cat food go missing from the supermarket?' Mo whispered.

The officer took a step closer, and Oli realised that up close he didn't quite look normal. His eyes were red-rimmed, his skin weirdly pale.

There was something else too: the way his face seemed totally absent of emotion, like a robot, cold and merciless.

The kind of person that might do *anything*.

On Oli's right, Sophia started to slowly raise her hands towards her head, and the torch fastened there.

'I'll ask you one last time,' the man growled, his own hand snaking towards the handcuffs on his belt. 'What are you doing here?'

The next few seconds felt to Oli as if they took place in slow motion. The policeman sneezed, and a thick, dark trickle of *something* burst out of one nostril. He reached up, knuckling the liquid away, but everyone saw the smear on the back of his hand.

Whatever had dripped from his nose was black and slimy.

Just like the slugs.

Just like the footprints in the classroom.

Just like the thing that had invaded Alex's house the previous night.

14

AMONG US

The police officer lunged, but he was a heartbeat too slow.

The instant he moved, Sophia pressed the button and a blinding light burst out of her torch, the glare aimed straight at the officer's face. He stumbled backwards, roaring in pain.

And then everyone ran.

This time they had the dawn light to guide their scramble through Howlmoor as night slid into day, the shadows slowly retreating. Alex found himself leading the way, the rest of the group trailing behind him. He didn't plan it, but his feet took him towards the bridge they'd crossed minutes before. His breath came in hot stabs, with the yells and cries of the others ringing in his ears. He chanced a look back and saw the officer smashing through the trees like they were barely there, slamming branches aside with his fists.

Alex's mind raced as he continued towards the bridge.

What the hell was going on?

He'd known things were about to turn bad the moment he'd seen the tin of cat food, the same kind of cat food that had sat empty in Alison's recycling crate. And when the black snot had burst out from the man's nose, exactly the same as the stuff his neighbour had wiped on her sleeve, things had started to slot into place. The meteorite, the break-ins, the black slime, the weird figure that had broken into his room, and now this, a police officer who was acting like some kind of superpowered axe murderer. There must be an explanation for it all, but Alex knew now wasn't the time to try to figure it out.

The five of them were almost across the bridge when the officer caught hold of Mo. The last member of their group was also the slowest, and Mo yelped in fright as the man's hand grabbed hold of his collar, dragging him off his feet and holding him up in the air as if he weighed nothing at all. Mo tried to get free, but he was going nowhere.

Alex skidded to a halt, not sure what to do. On his right, Oli stopped too, pulling out his super soaker and looking doubtfully at the trigger.

'I'm not sure this is going to help!' he cried, watching a lazy trail of water trickle uselessly out of the end. 'What do we do?'

Riley slid to a halt on the wooden bridge, watching Mo's face twist with fear.

'We can't just leave him!' she cried.

The next thing Alex knew, he was tossing his skateboard to one side and running back over the bridge, straight towards Mo and the police officer. He didn't have a plan, or any idea what he was going to do when he got there, but his mind had already decided that this was the only course of action. Mo had twisted round and was frantically wriggling like a fish on the end of a line.

'Please, let me go!' cried Mo, tears in his eyes. 'I won't tell anyone about the black snot, or the cat food! I'll pretend I never saw it! Just –'

Alex heard a roar escape from his lungs as he crashed into the police officer. It was like hitting a brick wall. Alex bounced off, landing on his backside with a meaty thud, a low creaking sound growing louder beneath him. The officer dropped Mo, switching his attention to Alex. But before the man could grab his new victim, Alex realised that his charge had had an unexpected side effect. Underneath them, their combined weight was causing the rotten struts of the bridge to give way.

A loud crack sounded above the gurgle of the river as their part of the bridge collapsed entirely, empty air suddenly underneath the policeman's feet. Alex was a fraction quicker than the officer and he leaped away, watching the policeman start to fall.

Except he wasn't quite quick enough.

One flailing hand clutched the front of Alex's hoodie. Alex tried to pull free, but he was caught fast. He felt himself being pulled downwards, towards the rushing torrent of Misty Creek. Alex experienced a terrible moment of weightlessness, saw the river looming up at him . . .

Until he was suddenly pulled up by his hood.

Alex heard the fabric rip, the seams stretching and tearing as he found himself caught in a terrifying tug of war between the officer and his friends, who had joined forces to rescue him. The front of Alex's hoodie gave way and he watched helplessly as the policeman slipped free, falling down towards the water. A moment later Oli and the others were hauling Alex up, the hard edge of the wooden bridge biting into his shins as he scrambled back to safety.

The police officer wasn't so lucky. He hit the surface of Misty Creek with a huge splash before the current swept him away.

'Thank you!' gasped Alex, struggling back to his feet. He peered over the side of the bridge, watching the man struggle and thrash as the freezing water carried him along.

'We have to go after him,' exclaimed Sophia, watching the dark figure of the officer as he clung desperately to a tree branch, the water threatening to pull him under.

'What if he's all . . . slimy?' asked Mo, rubbing at his chafed neck.

'He's right,' agreed Oli. 'That guy was unstoppable, like the Terminator or something. What if he comes after us again?'

'What if he *drowns*?' countered Sophia, looking from one face to another.

The last few words seemed to snap everyone back into action. They couldn't let him die, even if he did leak black alien slime and chase them through the woods. They trampled down from the bridge and ran along the sloping river banks, going to the officer's aid, but the branch he was clinging to snapped just as he came into sight, and he vanished into the frothy mass of white water once again. Alex led the way through the undergrowth, desperately scanning for any sign of him as they followed the creek through the forest. Faint beams of sunlight glinted on the surface of the water as day fully arrived, turning the water to fire.

A moment later Alex spotted a bedraggled figure washed up on a shady shale beach at the side of the creek. The officer's hat was gone, but there was no doubt who it was. The man wasn't moving.

Alex froze, any fear replaced by worry.

What if he'd accidentally killed the man?

All he'd meant to do was save Mo, not hurt anyone.

Sophia pushed past him, scrambling down onto the shore, and Alex raced after her.

'What do we do?' stuttered Mo as they gathered around the officer's still form. Alex's mouth went dry as he noticed that the man wasn't breathing, the rise and fall of his chest absent.

'We have to resuscitate him,' Riley said, rolling him onto his back. 'My grandad isn't well, and I know basic first aid, just in case.'

'She's right!' agreed Sophia. 'Clear his airway and give him mouth-to-mouth.'

'After he's been eating cat food?' protested Oli, backing away. 'Someone else gets that job!'

Mo's horrified squeal made them all switch their attention towards the officer's face. The man's eyes were still closed, his skin waxy, but that wasn't what had made Mo cry out.

It was the thing that was slithering out of his nose.

Eyes wide with horror, Alex watched as a fat black shape plopped out from one of the officer's nostrils, leaving a slimy trail behind it.

'What the hell is *that*?' murmured Oli, putting his hand over his own nose as if the creature was about to launch a slow-motion attack on him.

'It's one of those slug things,' Sophia exclaimed, a hint of awe to her words. 'It's just like the one I told you all about. It looks like a real slug. But it isn't!'

'What do we do with it?' Alex heard himself ask.

This time no one had an answer. The slug wriggled across the man's face, twitching and shivering, three long, thin antennae guiding the way.

'Do we . . . tread on it?' asked Oli. 'Squish it?'

Before anyone could respond, the slug plopped off the officer's face and landed on the shale at the river's edge. Its slow progress was illuminated by the rays of sunlight that were creeping through the trees, the orange glow coating the forest as the creature crawled to freedom.

Except it didn't get very far.

They all jumped as the slug suddenly exploded with a loud popping noise. A large, gooey chunk of it landed on the arm of Mo's sweater, causing him to wail in alarm.

'That's the grossest thing I've ever seen,' whispered Sophia in wonder, picking up a stick and using it to jab at what had landed on Mo. On the ground there was nothing left of the slug but a melting, smouldering mess.

'Could you quit the science experiment and just get it off me, please?' Mo begged, retrieving a tissue from his pocket.

A coughing sound made them all twist round, and they scrambled to their feet as the police officer belched a huge puddle of water onto the shore. He looked up at Alex and the others in confusion, as if he couldn't quite work out where he was, then slumped back onto the shale.

'You have to stop it,' he croaked, his words barely a whisper, his whole body shaking and convulsing. 'It's here, in Shiver Point, among us. It's taking the adults, one by one. That's . . . that's what it did to me!'

Sophia crouched down and tried to help the man into a sitting position.

'*What's* in Shiver Point?' she asked. '*What's* taking the adults?'

The officer coughed again, his body sagging with exhaustion. 'The children . . . it wants the children. A few hours, that's all we have.' He jabbed a trembling finger up towards the sky. 'You need to . . . you have to . . .'

He didn't manage any more. His eyes closed, the life seeping out of him as he fell unconscious.

'Is he . . . is he dead?' asked Alex. He couldn't even begin to unpick everything the man had just said.

Riley placed a hand on the man's chest. 'He's alive. But his heartbeat is weak. We need to get him to hospital.'

Sophia pulled out her phone, growling in frustration as she tried and failed to get a signal.

'If we follow the creek, sooner or later we'll hit the seafront,' Riley exclaimed. 'I'll go ahead, see if I can flag a car down. You guys try to carry him out!'

She dashed away into the trees, swallowed by the forest.

'What was that?' whispered Sophia as the rest of them caught their breath. 'What's going on in Shiver Point?'

'Aliens,' replied Oli, a smug tone to his voice. 'Is what happened back there proof enough for you, or do you still need that photographic evidence?'

'No, I think that's more than enough,' Sophia muttered, an apologetic look on her face. 'But from what that police officer just said, we need to figure out what it's doing here, and quickly.'

15

ON OUR OWN

If Sophia had thought that they'd be able to convince the grown-ups in Shiver Point that something bad was happening, she was quickly proven wrong. When she tried to tell one of the paramedics who'd arrived to treat the policeman about the rock that had fallen from the sky, he didn't even bother to hide the disbelief on his face.

'Aliens? In Shiver Point? What's wrong with you kids?'

Between the remaining four of them they'd managed to half carry, half drag the unconscious man to the edge of Howlmoor while Riley went ahead and flagged down a car, which had raced to the hospital to raise the alarm. By the time the gang emerged from the woodland, an ambulance was squealing into sight.

As the ambulance crew had treated the stricken officer, Sophia and the others had watched nervously, hoping he was going to be OK. But when things had finally calmed down and the man was in a stable condition, the focus had suddenly switched to how it had all happened. And despite the initial story the gang had agreed on, that they'd seen him fall in the river and gone to his rescue, Sophia had found herself deviating from their plan and spilling everything to the paramedic.

'We're not making this up. There was something . . . up his nose,' she persisted. 'This weird black creature, like a slug. But *not* a slug. And two weeks ago we saw a meteorite, right here in –'

'This thing from up his nose,' the paramedic cut in, giving Sophia a cold, flat look, 'where is it now?'

'It popped,' announced Oli, shaking his head in disbelief. 'It started to slither away and then just blew up . . . like a grenade on *Fortnite*.'

The paramedic switched his attention to Oli, folding his arms like a disapproving teacher. 'Blew up?' he repeated with a sigh. '*Right*. Look, you kids did well in saving this poor guy. Don't go ruining it by making up some silly stories.'

Sophia felt a rush of colour to her cheeks. It was something that always happened to her when she felt there was an injustice, like the time her Year 6 teacher had accused her of cheating after getting full marks in a test three times in a row.

'But we're not –'

Alex grabbed her arm, shaking his head. 'They're not going to believe us,' he whispered. 'No matter what you say. Like it or not, we're going to have to figure this out on our own.'

Sophia knew he was right, so she abandoned the argument. The paramedic crew got the officer onto a stretcher and loaded him into the back of their vehicle, and a few minutes later the ambulance pulled away, its blue lights blinking.

Sophia watched it go, replaying the events in the forest. Questions bounced around her head, but she couldn't find any kind of answers.

The crowd of dog walkers and joggers that had gathered to investigate the commotion started to drift away, all apart from one little huddle. Sophia winced as she noticed Bethany Blight hovering and clicking photos on her phone, a mischievous smile on her face. No doubt what had happened would be all over the internet once it was back up and running, with Bethany's spin on things making Sophia and the rest of them look even worse.

Riley had just suggested that they all go home when Damian Thorn arrived. He always looked the same, Sophia thought, like he'd been stitched into the scruffy brown suit he wore. His face had a pinched, inquisitive look to it as well, sort of like a rat, as he tried to sniff out a story to gobble down. This time it was Sophia and the others he was eyeing up for his next meal.

'The ambulance driver told me you were the ones who saved the police officer,' Thorn began in his nasal voice, aiming his microphone in

Sophia's direction. 'Why were you in the forest so early?'

Sophia had many skills, but lying wasn't one of them. She opened her mouth to answer, hoping something else would emerge before the truth.

'Birdwatching,' answered Mo for her, gesturing to the binoculars around his neck.

Thorn pulled a doubtful face. 'All of you?'

'We're in a club,' replied Oli, looking like he didn't quite believe it himself. 'We watch birds together all the time. Crows, owls . . . ostriches.'

Thorn's eyes lingered on Oli's hoodie, which had the words 'Frag Addict' emblazoned across the chest in huge fiery letters.

Sophia thought that the more time she spent with him, the more she realised that there was more to Oli than met the eye, although she was fairly sure that hiding in the reeds to spot birds wasn't one of his pastimes.

'I saw you at the supermarket earlier this week, after the break-in,' Thorn continued, keeping his focus on Oli. 'You're one of Chris Foster's sons, aren't you?'

'So?' replied Oli, suddenly defensive.

'So it wouldn't be the first time your family was involved in something they shouldn't have been.'

'What's that supposed to mean?' blurted Alex, an angry look on his face as he came to Oli's defence.

Thorn abandoned his microphone and pulled out a tattered-looking notebook, leafing through what was written there. 'You all go to Point Academy, don't you?'

Sophia gave a hesitant nod. She could already see where this line of questioning was going.

'How much do you know about the break-in there and the stolen computers?' Thorn continued.

'Our lessons in the computer room were cancelled,' Riley offered, 'but that's all we know.'

'Yeah,' added Oli. 'The less time I spend at school, the better.'

Thorn scribbled a few words in his jotter, like he'd just stumbled onto an important clue. Sophia found herself worrying if people found her notepad as irritating as she found Thorn's.

'So you don't like school?' countered Thorn. 'Were you happy when ICT got cancelled?'

Oli opened his mouth to reply, but Sophia had a feeling that whatever he said would just make things worse. She decided it was time to take charge.

'So what's *your* theory on things?' she fired at Thorn.

The reporter looked confused for a moment and flipped through his notes again, as if searching for an answer there. 'Well, let's see. A series of break-ins, the stolen cat food, that weird smell around town. I think a group of teenagers are probably to blame.' He narrowed his eyes at them.

'Well, we're only twelve,' answered Sophia, gesturing towards the others. 'So it couldn't have been us. Goodbye, Mr Thorn.'

She didn't wait for a reply. She nodded to the others and like a sergeant major led them all away from the forest in the direction of Shiver Point.

16

BODYSNATCHERS

It was already warm in the treehouse, fingers of sunlight shining through the windows, but Alex couldn't seem to stop shivering. After checking in with their parents and coming up with a suitable homework-related cover story to explain why they'd been out so early, the gang had reconvened back at Riley's.

But none of them knew what to do now.

'Maybe we ignore it, bury our heads in the sand, hope it all goes away,' suggested Mo.

Riley rubbed at her eyes. She looked tired, but then Alex reckoned they all did after spending the entire night prowling around Howlmoor.

'So, what?' she said between yawns. 'You think you're just going to be able to forget what you saw last night?'

Mo grew pale at the question. 'I guess not. In fact, I think I'll probably be seeing that slug in my dreams for the foreseeable future. If I ever manage to get to sleep again.'

Sophia had her notebook out again, her pen moving swiftly as she transcribed the events of the night.

'It had to have been the slug,' she said, her pen squeaking to a momentary halt. 'One minute the police officer was attacking us, the next he was a different person. Could it . . . could the slug have affected him somehow?'

Alex shivered as he pictured the slug slithering out of the man's nostril like a slimy black cocktail sausage. Like Mo, he wasn't sure he'd ever forget it, or be able to eat party food again. 'I think you're right, Sophia. The way that officer acted wasn't normal. But where are the slugs coming from? What do they want?'

On the other side of the treehouse, Oli was crunching his way through a mammoth pack of Roast Beef Monster Munch. He held one of the misshapen crisps up into the light thoughtfully. 'And how many other people in Shiver Point have also got those yucky black things up their nose?'

Alex's mind flashed back to his neighbour, Alison, and the dark trickle he was sure he'd seen her wipe from her nostrils.

'It all has to somehow be linked to that figure who came to my house,' he said. 'It was surrounded by the slugs, and they only turned up after we saw that meteorite come down in the woods.'

'Maybe we should tell our parents,' suggested Mo.

Sophia gave a defiant shake of her head. 'That paramedic didn't believe me. I don't think our parents would either. Worst-case scenario, they ground us, lock us in our rooms and then we can't do anything.' She fell quiet for a moment, her blue eyes glazed over. 'That police officer said that something was here, in town. *Among us*. But why?'

Oli threw his empty packet of crisps down onto the floorboards, where the wrapper slowly unfurled. 'Maybe it's like one of those bodysnatcher films,' he mumbled, sucking on his fingers. At their confused expressions he sat up straight, his eyes wide. 'Don't *any* of you guys watch horror films?'

'For some reason our parents don't let us watch films that could corrupt our young minds and give us nightmares for years to come.'

Oli shrugged at Sophia's comment and wiped his fingers on his jeans. 'That's a shame. You guys are really missing out. Anyway, there's loads of films out there where an alien life form takes over human bodies. They're pretty scary, like this one where . . .'

Alex raised his eyebrows as Oli went into very graphic detail about a recent horror movie he'd watched. When he finally finished telling the story, Alex shook his head, trying to rid his mind of the terrifying details. 'To be honest, I'm still struggling with the concept of aliens being real.'

'Even after the slug?' asked Mo, who seemed to have been similarly affected by Oli's tale, if his bloodless face was anything to go by.

'Even after the slug.'

'*Anyway,*' Oli continued, ignoring the other two, 'in most bodysnatcher films, aliens take over a town, slowly infiltrating every home, possessing everybody.' He stopped and took a deep breath, the enthusiasm fading from his eyes. 'The problem is, those films never have a happy ending.'

Mo started to chew at his bottom lip. 'How *do* they end?'

Oli retrieved his empty crisp packet, looking longingly at the crumbs inside. 'The alien usually wins.'

Alex and Riley exchanged a grimace.

'Well,' announced Sophia, clicking the end of her pen in and out, 'this time we need to make sure they don't. So first things first, we need to figure out what this alien wants with Shiver Point.'

'The children,' Alex answered, thinking back to the police officer's panicked face after he'd been rescued from the river and the slug had burst. 'The police officer said it wanted the children.'

'Doesn't that mean *us*?' asked Mo, casting a nervous look towards the rolled-up rope ladder that kept them safe from anyone below.

Over on her workbench, Riley had produced a map of Shiver Point and she traced a finger along the lines that made up their little town. 'I use this sometimes when I'm trying to work out how much range I can get on the walkie-talkies. That tunnel we saw in Howlmoor . . . Where does it lead? And why was the officer down there?'

'Narnia?' suggested Oli hopefully.

Sophia shot him an exasperated look. 'You get to Narnia through a wardrobe, not a creaky gate in the forest. But Riley's right. If we want to know what the alien wants, we need to find out what that officer was doing down there. Which means we need to find out where that tunnel leads to.'

Alex looked down at his phone, scowling at the persistent lack of signal. 'Looks like Google's still out of the question.'

Sophia slipped her notebook into her blazer pocket and pulled something else out. It looked suspiciously like a library card. 'The internet isn't the only way to find things out. All the stuff we want to know will be available at Shiver Point library.'

Riley was staring up at the treehouse wall, at a funky clock she'd made out of cogs from various clockwork mechanisms. 'It's ten o'clock on a Sunday morning. Isn't the library closed all day?'

'For everyone else, maybe,' answered Sophia in a self-satisfied voice. 'But me and Ms Stoker are best buddies.'

'Who's that?' asked Oli. 'Dracula's wife?'

Sophia rolled her eyes, her favourite thing to do when it came to Oli. 'Ms Stoker's our town's librarian. I spend a lot of time in the library at weekends. In fact, I pretty much live there. I help with deliveries, laminate book covers and –'

'The library?' echoed Oli in an awestruck tone, as if he'd never realised such places existed. 'Should we all come?'

Sophia gave him a doubtful look. 'I'm . . . I'm not sure how . . . *useful* you'd be in a library.'

'So what should the rest of us do?' asked Mo.

Sophia studied him for a moment then nodded to herself. 'You – you're coming with me, Mo. The rest of you take a walk around Shiver Point. See if anything else seems out of the ordinary.'

'Apart from the possessed humans, the giant slugs and the fact that the air smells like the toilet after my dad's been in there?' asked Oli, his eyes fixed on the town in the distance.

Sophia rose to her feet, gesturing with her index finger for Mo to do the same. Before they made it to the treehouse doorway, Alex called them back. He still didn't understand what they'd stumbled into, but he had the feeling it was up to their little gang to stop it.

'Be careful,' he warned them. 'And don't trust anyone.'

17

STUDY TIME

Mo had never been sure about libraries. There was something undeniably creepy about them.

It wasn't just the smell, or the quiet, or the thought that some of the books must be hundreds of years old, and have been last leafed through by people that had been dead for decades. It was more the odd sensation that someone was watching, hidden in the aisles, just waiting for a chance to jump out from the shadows.

Mo knew it was his imagination.

But under the current circumstances, the feeling was worse than ever.

It didn't help that Ms Stoker was more than a little eccentric. Shiver Point's bubbly librarian had bright pink hair and wore a thick fur coat, even inside. Underneath her jacket she wore a *Goonies* T-shirt, and around her neck hung a pair of oversized headphones, with a wire hanging down to what she had told him was a CD Walkman. Mo wasn't even sure you could buy CDs any more, except maybe from the charity shop. When Ms Stoker wasn't singing along to her tunes, she was popping the gum in her mouth like a machine gun. But even if she was a bit odd, Mo reckoned Ms Stoker was better than the school librarian at Point Academy, who didn't seem to know any word other than 'shush' and who let her cats roam free in the aisles, hissing if any student got too close to them or dared to touch the wrong book.

Maybe she was an upgrade on the school librarian, but Ms Stoker hadn't stopped chattering as she'd led them down to the library's basement. 'People are getting worried about all the things going on in town, but nothing ever happens in Shiver Point,' she'd mused. 'In some places you hear stories about vampires, skinwalkers, even the odd poltergeist, but in this town all we get is stolen vegetables. Or so most people think . . .'

She gave Mo a knowing wink, as if the two of them were in on a secret together, and then paused at the bottom of the stone steps, clicking on a light switch that dimly illuminated an underground chamber full of filing cabinets and shelves that stretched as far as Mo could see.

'This is where we keep the town records and the archives of all the old newspapers,' Ms Stoker explained. 'What exactly is it you're looking for?'

Sophia shrugged nonchalantly. 'Oh, just . . . something for our geography homework. It's to do with the old tunnels that run under Shiver Point. It's all very boring.'

Ms Stoker looked at Sophia like she wasn't quite convinced, but if she was suspicious she kept it to herself. 'Well, if it's town schematics you want, I'd start with the map section down in aisle four. Be careful if you go into the tunnels – you never know what you might find down there.'

There was something strange about the librarian, Mo reckoned: she had a twinkle in her eye as if she knew a little bit more about Shiver Point than she was letting on.

'Don't worry,' he assured her. 'There's no way we want to go *into* the tunnels. We just need to find out a little more about where they go to.'

Ms Stoker brushed a flurry of cobwebs off a nearby desk and retreated towards the stairs. 'Well, I'll leave you two to it. If you need me, I'll be upstairs.'

Mo suppressed a shiver as the librarian's footsteps faded away. 'I don't like it down here,' he said, casting a gloomy look towards the darkened aisles. 'It's cold and it smells funny.'

'Concentrate,' snapped Sophia, leading him towards the row Ms Stoker had indicated. 'It's a library, not a morgue.'

'I'm not sure what the difference is,' he mumbled, following her like an unhappy puppy. 'Why did you even bring me here? I'm the least useful person in the group.'

Sophia paused, giving Mo a thoughtful look. 'You've been in my classes since primary school. I know you don't think so, but you're clever.

Nearly as clever as I am. And two minds are better than one.'

Mo was happy with the compliment, but it didn't make him feel much better. The next two hours involved him jumping at every creak of the shelves as the two of them searched through set after set of huge folders crammed with maps and archived documents. He wished he'd stayed in the treehouse, chatting to the others, or even better, gone for a sleep. It was so creepy down in the library stacks that when he started to get hungry, even the rumble of his own stomach made him jump.

Mo was just about to suggest that they abandon their search and head back to the land of the living when Sophia snapped upright, jabbing her finger towards the map she had just unrolled, which had dozens of coloured lines scrawled across the page.

'Found it!' she announced in triumph.

'Does that mean we can go now?'

'Not yet,' Sophia replied, pulling out her phone and taking several pictures of the paper in front of her. 'This is a map of the tunnels under Shiver Point. And here . . .'

She took hold of another huge sheet of paper she had lying nearby and dragged it on top of the first. 'If we put the map of the tunnels over the town plan . . .'

She went quiet, tracing the lines on the sheets.

'That tunnel we found in Howlmoor leads to the sewers,' she announced gleefully. 'And the sewers go all over town, like a spider's web.'

'Didn't you say you saw one of those slugs by a drain on the way to school?'

Sophia stared up towards the ceiling, where a hanging bare bulb shivered and blinked.

'That's right. So those slug things must be down in the sewers, under the town. That must be where they're coming from, and how they're infecting people all over Shiver Point.'

Outside the wind howled, the moan shuddering through the old building.

'What if . . . what if they're not alone? What if that thing that broke into Alex's house is down there too?' asked Mo.

Sophia rolled the map back up, replacing it among the others on the shelves. 'One problem at a time. We need to go back, tell the others what we've found, and work out what to do next, but before we do . . .' She paused, took a deep breath and rubbed her eyes in frustration. 'It's like I'm missing something. Like there's something in front of me that I can't quite see. While we're here, I want to look at one more thing.'

'I was worried you'd say that,' moaned Mo. 'What do we have to research now?'

Sophia consulted her notes, staring at two words scribbled there in pink pen, the letters underlined and followed by a series of question marks.

'Cat food.'

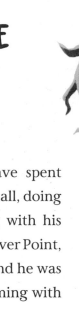

18

NOTHING TO SEE HERE

Back in his old life, Alex would have spent Sunday morning hanging out at the mall, doing tricks in the skate park and chilling with his friends. Instead he found himself in Shiver Point, which offered none of those things. And he was pretty sure his old home wasn't swarming with aliens either.

As he walked the streets with Oli and Riley, hoping to find more clues for their investigation, it felt as if Shiver Point was holding its breath, waiting for something to happen, even if it didn't know what. The people he saw, pushing prams and carrying shopping bags and making their way to the gym, seemed nervous somehow. They glanced frequently at their watches, kept their distance from each other and moved swiftly to their destinations, as if to stay too long in one place spelled danger. Alex couldn't help but think back to his mum, and how she'd been asleep this morning when he'd popped home. He'd hated leaving her again, especially with slug-nosed Alison next door and the knowledge that more and more townsfolk were being infected.

And what if that creature from two nights ago came back, looking for Alex but finding his mum?

But right now he didn't have a choice.

They needed to find answers, and fast.

'What exactly are we looking for?' Oli asked, kicking a stone across the pavement so hard that it bounced off the kerb, flew into the air and nearly hit a scavenging pigeon.

If he was honest, Alex didn't know. It wasn't as if there was a trail of extraterrestrial slugs making their way slowly through town, or a neon sign that screamed 'slimy aliens here'.

'Maybe we'll know it when we see it,' answered Riley, checking the signal on her walkie-talkie before clipping it back onto her belt.

'Let's hope so,' muttered Oli, yawning theatrically.

They made their way along the main street, peering into shop windows. Their aim was to try to spot anything out of the ordinary, just as Sophia had suggested, but Alex got the distinct feeling they were wasting their time. They ventured into two of the general stores, looking to see if either had any cat food in stock, but both were sold out. Alex wasn't sure if that was a good sign or not.

'Food,' moaned Oli as they walked past a pasty shop. 'Why do we keep seeing places that sell food?'

He stroked his tummy mournfully, like it hadn't seen food for days, but Alex had already watched him gobble down a packet of sandwiches from the garage followed by a huge packet of Quavers. As the morning dragged on, Alex was starting to understand why Oli got into so much trouble at school. If it wasn't the smell of food making him drift off task, it was the bright colours of posters outside the Night Owl for new movies that caught his eye. Oli had a lot of energy, but Alex reckoned it was just a case of him needing to channel it in the right way.

The three of them were just about to give up and head back to the treehouse when things suddenly turned sinister. As they passed the town hall, Riley pointed out the mayor, who was at the top of the steps sticking up posters to advertise that evening's meeting.

'Should we take a closer look?' suggested Riley, pointing towards the towering columns covered in posters.

'I haven't got any better ideas,' Alex replied.

It turned out there was nothing that seemed out of place on any of the posters; they simply detailed the start time and encouraged all Shiver Point residents, adults and children alike, to attend. Alex was just about to suggest they call it a day when the mayor spotted them and waddled over. His red official cloak billowed behind him, catching in the breeze.

'Are you coming tonight?' he asked, jabbing a meaty finger towards one of the posters.

'Erm . . . we're not sure,' answered Riley, looking towards the boys for support.

'Yeah, six thirty might be . . . past my bedtime,' Oli said.

When the mayor gave Oli a doubtful look, Alex noticed how unwell the man seemed. His eyes were red-rimmed, a film of sweat shone on his brow and his laboured breathing gave Alex flashbacks to being chased by the policeman.

'Well, you should,' insisted the mayor. 'We don't want you missing the fun, do we?'

There was something off about the way the man was behaving, Alex decided. It was there, in the odd glint in his eye, the sly, secretive smile that danced on his lips. Evidently Riley sensed it too, grabbing hold of Alex's sleeve and starting to pull him back down the steps.

The mayor kept his beady eyes focused on them for a moment longer, as if they were a tantalising snack left on the side of his plate. Just as Alex started to back away he felt his eyes widen in fear. A slow black trickle slid from one of the mayor's nostrils, glistening like oil in the sunlight.

'We have to get going,' Alex stammered, clutching Oli's hood and dragging him along too.

'Did you see that?' he babbled as soon as they stumbled to the bottom of the stairs.

'You bet I did,' replied Oli. 'I think I've finally lost my appetite.'

Riley leaned in closer so that her words couldn't be heard by any townsfolk that passed them.

'He's one of them too, isn't he?' she whispered, her eyes darting around as if she was no longer sure who she could trust. 'Like the police officer, like your neighbour, Alex. He's all . . .'

'Sluggy?' offered Oli, probing one of his nostrils as if worried that one of the slimy creatures had somehow managed to slither in while he wasn't looking. Alex knew the feeling.

'That's one way to put it,' Riley answered. 'But if those slugs are taking over Shiver Point one adult at a time, what do they want? And what's going to happen next?'

Alex chanced a look back over his shoulder and saw the mayor watching them go, his long

147

cloak billowing around him making him look like the Grim Reaper.

'I don't know,' he answered, unclipping the walkie-talkie from where it was fastened onto his belt to radio the others. 'But we need to figure it out quickly.'

19

THE SOLUTION

It was mid-afternoon by the time the group reconvened at the treehouse. After a night exploring the forest followed by a morning investigating the town, Riley and the others were exhausted, but there was no way any of them were in the mood to sleep.

'What did you find?' Riley asked as Mo and Sophia clambered back inside the treehouse, reeling in the ladder behind them. Beyond the windows, Shiver Point looked calm and tranquil, the sunlight glinting off the harbour in the distance.

'The bad news first,' Sophia announced. 'We popped into the hospital to ask about the police officer. He's fine, which is good, but he doesn't remember anything, which means there's no way we can get any more information from him.'

'Not a thing?' asked Alex.

Sophia shook her head, pulling out her phone and passing it to the others so that they could see the photographs she and Mo had taken. 'Now the better news: that tunnel we found leads into the sewers, miles and miles of them, that run under Shiver Point. From the smell, and the slug I saw by the drain last week, I think those yucky black creatures must be down there, using the tunnel system to get all over the town.'

Oli rubbed at his eyes, punctuating his question with a huge yawn. 'So if they live down in the sewers, how are they infecting people?'

Riley studied the images on Sophia's phone then passed it back to its owner. 'Maybe they come out in the night, go into people's houses and slither up their noses while they're asleep.'

'That's disgusting,' declared Alex.

'Better than them coming up the toilet while you're sitting on it and . . .' Oli didn't finish his sentence, leaving the others to fill in the gaps.

'Ugh!' cried Mo. 'I'm going to need enough counselling in Student Support as it is after this without you filling my head with even worse images!'

'Either way, I think we're going to have to go down into the sewers,' said Sophia, sticking her phone back into her pocket and getting the conversation back on track. Riley was grateful.

Mo fired her a horrified look. 'Do we have to?'

'Yeah,' answered Alex. 'I think we do. After what the police officer said, after the warning he gave us, I don't think we have a choice.'

Mo looked from one face to the next, a flicker of uncertainty in his eyes. 'What if . . . what if there's something *else* down there? Aside from the slugs. What if that thing that broke into Alex's house is there?'

Oli nodded thoughtfully. 'Like a level boss.'

Sophia turned to him. She had her notebook out again, Riley noticed, making notes like a super-efficient secretary. 'What does that even mean?'

151

'Well,' Oli started, clearly loving the fact that for once he knew more about something than the others, 'in a video game, once you beat the minions, you have to beat the boss. So the Nemesis in *Resident Evil*, or Giovanni in *Pokémon Go*.'

'But this isn't a video game,' Sophia pointed out.

'Well, let's hope not,' muttered Oli, flashing an evil grin at her, 'because usually the brain is the character that gets killed off first.'

'What else did you find out?' asked Riley, trying to move things forward before an argument broke out.

'Not much,' answered Sophia, firing a hostile look towards Oli. 'Mo and I researched into cat food, but we didn't find much.' She paused, the pages of her notebook fluttering as she leafed through it. 'Cat food is made up of ground meat and eggs. It also contains calcium, magnesium and a load of vitamin E.'

'In English?' asked Alex.

'It's super healthy, but it tastes gross. And it doesn't explain why it all got stolen from the supermarket, or why that police officer was munching away on a can of it.'

'Although maybe that officer explains how so much of it went missing,' Alex suggested. 'He was so strong he could probably lift a pallet of it all on his own.'

Riley's mind drifted back to a few weeks ago, to a lesson they'd had on vitamins, how certain ones were essential to a person's wellbeing. Like Mo, Riley enjoyed science, and how it always had definitive answers, and the lessons tended to stick in her head.

'Wait – vitamin A helps your immunity and skin, right, and vitamin D is good for teeth and bones? But doesn't . . . doesn't vitamin E protect you from sunlight?' she wondered aloud.

Sophia turned slowly to face Riley, like she'd just said something in a different language. 'What did you say?'

Riley shrugged. 'It was in Mrs Taylor's class a few weeks ago. I think you were absent from that lesson, showing some guests around the school.'

Sophia slapped her forehead as she came to the same conclusion Riley had drawn. 'Why didn't I see it?' she groaned.

'See what?' asked Mo, glancing from one of the girls to the other.

Sophia stood up and paced to one of the treehouse windows, where the sun was starting its slow descent towards the horizon. 'Think about it – we've only ever seen that figure at night. The way that police officer pointed up at the sky, like he was trying to tell us something . . . The stolen cat food . . . How those slugs both popped as soon as they got caught by the light . . .'

'Are you going to tell us what you're talking about?' asked Oli. 'Or are you just going to keep being super annoying?'

'Sunlight!' Sophia exclaimed, turning back towards the others and grinning at Riley. 'You're brilliant, Riley! Those slugs are vulnerable to *sunlight*! It was staring us in the face all along and we never saw it!'

'I don't get it,' drawled Oli, scratching at his curly hair like he was trying to solve a complex maths problem. 'How does cat food fit into all this?'

'Vitamin E protects you from sunlight, or rather it protects you from ultraviolet rays. My best guess is that the cat food was stolen by all the Shiver Point adults who've been infected, so that they can protect themselves, or rather the parasite inside them, when they're out in the open.'

It was all starting to fall into place, Riley reckoned, or at least some of the pieces were.

Mo turned to Alex, a nervous glint in his eyes. 'What did you guys find out in town?'

Alex shrugged. 'Not much. Except that the mayor's infected too. We saw that black stuff up his nose. He kept going on about the meeting tonight, and how important it was for us to come along.'

Mo stared at Alex like he'd just seen a ghost. 'It wants the children . . . isn't that what that police officer said? But why? I mean, we still don't know, do we?'

'Maybe that's a good thing,' Alex said. 'Maybe if we can stop whatever's out there, we'll never have to find out. I'm just relieved that my mum works nights, so she's safely out of the town when those things are hunting. And if Riley and Sophia are right, she's not in danger in the daytime, when those slugs can't come out.' Riley could see the relief in Alex's eyes at this revelation.

'But that officer, didn't he say that we don't have much time?' She slid her mind back to earlier that day, and the words the officer had gabbled before he'd fallen unconscious. She'd been so thrown by everything that had happened prior to that point, she'd barely registered much of what he'd said in the moment. But now it all came flooding back. 'Wait, you don't think . . .'

Sophia nodded, pulling out her phone and scrolling through the photographs she'd taken earlier, her face getting paler and paler.

'Oh no. No, no, no,' she mumbled.

'What?' demanded Oli.

'The sewers. There's a main intersection right under the town hall,' she explained, turning her phone around so that the others could see it. 'All the infected townsfolk have to do is lock the doors, turn off the lights, and it'll be . . .'

'A slugfest,' said Alex.

Riley shivered, trying not to picture what might happen in the huge auditorium once it went dark. Just one of the slugs was enough for her. A whole town hall full of them . . . Riley's brain tortured her by imagining the combination of slithering and screams as the slugs attacked.

'But our . . . our parents will be going to that meeting!' Mo protested, eyes wide with horror. 'We have to warn them!'

'You think they'll believe us?' Oli asked. 'If I go home and start ranting about giant slugs and aliens, I'll be kissing goodbye to my Xbox. We're just kids. No one will listen to us.'

'Then we don't have a choice,' Riley announced. 'We have to go down into the sewers and stop the slugs *before* the meeting happens!'

'And how do we do that?' protested Oli. 'Take a big bucket down there, fill it with slugs and drag them out into the sunlight before they manage to slither up into our brains?'

'No,' said Riley, turning to her workbench and digging through her tools. 'Maybe we can take the sunlight to the slugs.'

20

A BUNCH OF LOSERS

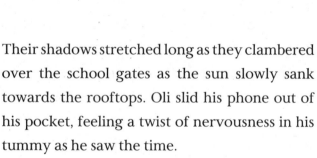

Their shadows stretched long as they clambered over the school gates as the sun slowly sank towards the rooftops. Oli slid his phone out of his pocket, feeling a twist of nervousness in his tummy as he saw the time.

Almost four o'clock.

Two hours until it was dark.

Two and a half hours until the meeting began, and the slugs that had taken over Shiver Point one adult at a time sprang their trap. Oli stuffed his phone back into his pocket and took a look around. Point Academy's playground was silent, the football field deserted, as if the idea of the place being full of children was just a dream. He stared at the empty classrooms that lined the field, trying to swallow down his fear. School wasn't his favourite place, but right now he'd give anything to be sitting behind a desk, listening to one of his teachers drone on.

He watched as Alex and Mo lifted up the manhole cover, holding his nose as the awful smell that hung over Shiver Point suddenly intensified. Riley took a step forward, shining her torch beam into the darkness below.

'I'm really not sure about this,' whispered Mo, wiping his fingers on the hem of his parka.

For once, Oli agreed with him.

The afternoon had gone by in a blur. Riley had powered into action at her bench, assisted with her new invention by Mo, while Sophia had studied the maps of the sewers. Meanwhile Alex had snuck off to leave a note for his mum, trying to persuade her not to go to the meeting.

Oli hadn't bothered. He was pretty sure that if he left a note back home, either one of his sisters would throw it in the bin or Cujo would eat it – he was probably starving after being put on half rations.

Based on the photographs of the maps that Sophia took at the library, they'd decided to enter the sewers via the manhole cover inside the school gates. As it was a Sunday, Sophia reckoned that the site would be deserted, and after being chased by the policeman in the forest, they all agreed that going in that way was far too risky.

But now the manhole cover was off and the way ahead was clear, none of the gang wanted to be the first to go down into the darkness.

'If we don't do this,' murmured Sophia, trying to rally herself, 'school might not reopen after half-term.'

Mo leaned forward, peering into the blackness below. 'It's dark down there,' he whispered. 'And smelly. And scary. And if we go down, we might never come out.'

From the lack of response, Oli reckoned everyone else felt the same way. The wind whistled across the playground, making him shiver. The sun was falling, slowly and steadily. Every second that passed brought the meeting closer, but going down into the sewers felt like a step too far.

A static hiss cut through the silence, the sudden sound echoing around the empty playground and making them all jump in fright. For a moment Oli couldn't work out where the sound came from, then he watched Riley unclip the walkie-talkie from her belt and give it a confused stare.

'I changed the channel to the one me and my grandad use,' she said, turning up the volume. 'I thought as we're all together now, I should –'

'Riley, can you hear me?' came a voice from the radio, cutting her off. *'It's Grandad here. Listen, if you can hear me, the local councillors have been knocking on doors around town telling everyone they have to attend the town hall meeting this evening, and that they need to bring their children too. I checked the treehouse and you aren't there, so I guess you're with your new friends somewhere. If you can hear this, can you come back home?'*

There was a pause, a moment of silence, then two last words.

'Love you. Over.'

'This is really happening, isn't it?' whispered Riley, a look of horror on her face.

161

Sophia nodded and took a hesitant step towards the manhole cover, giving the darkness a doubtful stare.

Oli knew how she felt. Now that he was actually here, his brain was torturing him with terrifying images of the kinds of creatures that could be lurking down there.

'Maybe we should just warn them,' suggested Mo, breathing on his fingertips as the wind blew again. 'Get to the town hall early, stand at the steps and tell everyone who turns up what's about to happen.'

Oli slumped down on a bench at the side of the playground. 'You think they'd actually believe us? *Us?* Look around. We're a bunch of losers, aren't we?' He took a deep breath, his finger moving from one member of the gang to the next. 'Mo, you're a nerd who's scared of his own shadow. Alex is a loner, who no one knows. Sophia's a brain whose only friend is that notebook of hers. Riley . . . I don't know what she is, some kind of genius inventor. And me . . . everyone knows what I am: I'm trouble. So no one's going to listen to us. If we tried to warn them, they'd laugh us out of town.'

'Or worse,' said Alex. 'If there's so many infected townsfolk now, wouldn't they just grab us before we could even get near the place?'

Mo looked towards the school gates, like he was ready to make a run for it. 'That police officer said whatever's behind this wants the children. We don't know what for, but that definitely means it wants *us*. Do we really want to go down into those sewers and say, "Hi, we're here!"?'

A cloud of defeat seemed to drift off the empty football field, enveloping the group. Oli watched the others slump to the ground one by one, their eyes fixed uncertainly on the abyss that was the manhole. All except for Riley. She cleared her throat, pushed back her shoulders and stepped in front of the group.

'You've all been in my treehouse. You ever wonder why it looks out over the graveyard, why my grandad chose to buy a cottage there?'

'Because he's got awful taste?' asked Oli with a smirk.

Riley slowly shook her head. 'No. My mum and dad died when I was little, and they're buried in that graveyard. My grandad bought the cottage, and let me have the treehouse, so that every morning, when I wake up, I'll feel close to them. But what I have now, all I have now, is my grandad. If he goes to that meeting, I'll lose him too. And I can't.'

She reached up, wiping a tear away from her dark eyes. 'I *can't*. And trust me, none of you want to lose your parents either. So we have to do this. Who's with me?'

Alex stood up, reaching out and taking Riley's hand. 'You're right. I'm not risking losing my mum. So I'm in.'

Riley gave Alex the kind of smile that made Oli feel a little jealous.

Mo watched the two of them, then he stumbled up alongside them, nibbling on his fingernail as he spoke. 'I've never been so scared, not ever, but I can't risk my parents either. My mum and dad would do anything for me, and if anything ever happened to my brother . . . I guess I'd even miss those smelly socks of his.'

Sophia smiled, rising to her feet. 'My two mums are the best. I don't even need to think about this.'

Oli was the last one to stand up, sighing as he gave his answer. 'I guess I'm in too, then. And being the middle child might suck, but nowhere near as much as not having any family at all would. But if I end up with one of those slugs living in my brain, I'm not going to be happy.'

Riley dug around in her backpack and drew out a strange rectangular black object, with a clear glass pipe in the centre that reminded Oli of a lightsabre.

'That isn't going to happen,' she announced. 'This is our secret weapon. We go down into those sewers, and we finish this.'

21

THE SEWERS

'I don't like it down here.' Mo shuddered as Oli pulled the sewer cover back across, banishing the daylight and blocking the world above from view. The only source of light was the faint glowing stripes from where drains studded the roof.

'If you wanted bright lights, popcorn and laughs, maybe you should have gone to the Night Owl,' grunted Oli, jumping down from the ladder that ran up the wall of the tunnel and grimacing as murky water splashed up his tracksuit bottoms.

Mo sighed, squinting as he tried to make

sense of the shadows that lay further along the tunnel.

'What's that noise?' he asked, not really sure himself which sound he was referring to. There were almost too many to count: the constant dripping of water from all around, the rumble of the cars on the roads in the distance, the scuttling of tiny creatures in the tunnels and the weird irregular bubbling sound that Mo was pretty sure indicated that someone in one of the hundreds of houses in Shiver Point was currently flushing the toilet.

'It's your inner you, telling you to be brave,' Riley answered, handing Mo a chunky-looking torch. 'Take this. I based it on a tactical military torch, just like soldiers have. It should last a whole weekend, not just the few hours we're down here, and it's twelve times brighter than a normal torch. Stay at the back, and make sure no one tries to creep up on us.'

'Doesn't the person at the back always get eaten?' asked Oli, a mischievous smile on his face.

'Not helpful, Oli!' snapped Sophia, throwing as comforting a smile as she could muster at Mo.

Alex sighed loudly, shining his torch along the circular sweep of the tunnel. 'Come on, you lot, we need to get a move on and head towards the town hall. There's miles of tunnels down here, and no way of knowing where those slugs are, or if we'll be able to make it before the meeting starts.'

'Can't we use the map?' asked Oli.

Sophia pulled out her phone, flicking through to the photographs of the sewer system she'd taken in the library.

'Some of it's in here, and the rest is up here,' she explained, tapping the side of her head with a finger.

'Isn't that a bad idea?' said Mo, reaching out to touch the slimy surface of the tunnel wall out of scientific curiosity and then quickly drawing back his hand with a shiver. 'I mean, if something happens to you, we're all lost.'

'Then we'd better look after her,' said Riley, pushing past the others and setting off into the darkness.

Below ground, time seemed to lose all sense of meaning. Mo felt as if the real world was miles away, rather than just a few metres above them. Water soaked his feet, edging up the legs of his trousers as he plodded through the thick dark slush. Every now and again they'd hear a squeal, or a scuttle, and lift their torches in time to glimpse a wiry pink tail, its bloated owner scrambling back into the shadows.

'This place is something else,' muttered Oli, pulling a face as a dead seagull drifted past, one beady eye seeming to focus on each of the children in turn. 'I don't usually get scared of anything except vegan food. But right now . . . right now I wish I hadn't watched that film about the killer clown that lives in the sewers.'

Mo hoped that nobody would ask for more details, and was more than relieved when their little group trudged on in silence.

Each tunnel seemed to look like the last. Their splashing footsteps echoed away into the darkness, the maze of sewers stretching on forever. Every time Mo glanced down at his watch he felt his breath catch at how much time had passed; the minutes were counting down quickly, like sand through an hourglass.

They'd been walking for almost an hour when Sophia finally stumbled to a halt.

'I'm . . . I'm sorry,' she stuttered. 'But I don't know where we are. The maps aren't accurate, and the tunnels, they're not where they're supposed to be. I think we're out near Elm Grove, just west of the town centre, but I don't can't be sure.'

In the torchlight, Mo could see the anguish on Sophia's face. She was the one who always knew the answers, who never got things wrong, and it was obvious how upset she was.

'I'm so sorry,' she repeated, looking down at her feet as if she wished she could teleport away. 'I've let you all down.'

'Don't be,' replied Alex, and he put a reassuring hand on her shoulder. 'You haven't. None of the rest of us would have a clue where we were. Let's face it, without you we wouldn't even have known where to begin.'

For a moment nobody spoke. Oli's tummy rumbled miserably, the sound echoing in the tunnel like a demented frog. The others giggled at the noise in spite of themselves, but the glum look on Oli's face made the moment turn serious.

'It's going to be dark soon,' he whispered. 'Maybe we should give up, go back, try to warn them after all.'

Riley shook her head, tears in her eyes, and Mo knew she must be picturing her grandad. 'We can't. We have to find those slugs and the thing that's making them, and get rid of it!'

Sophia sighed, staring down at the dirty water around her feet. 'We don't even know if that weapon you've made will work on them though. It was just my stupid theory, and if I was wrong about being able to find the way, maybe I was wrong about that too.'

'So, what, we're giving up?' asked Alex, an edge of anger in his voice.

'It wasn't my idea to come down here,' retorted Oli.

'I'm not sure you had any ideas at all,' snapped Sophia, her frustration giving way to annoyance.

Suddenly everyone was raising their voices, arguing, their little mismatched group falling to pieces in the stinky tunnel. Mo could see it, right in front of his eyes. These kids weren't strangers any more, or fellow pupils that ignored him all day in school. Somehow, over the past few days, they had become his friends. And he didn't want to lose them.

'Stop it!' he yelled, half scared that his voice would carry and attract danger. 'Just stop arguing! How's that going to help us?'

There was an abrupt silence, deafening in the darkness. Mo cleared his throat and looked from one face to the next.

'Listen to me. We have to go on. For Shiver Point, for all the people up there, but most of all for *us*. I've never had friends before. I've never had people like you guys who, who . . . who put up with me and notice me and don't dismiss everything I say the second it comes out of my mouth. I like hanging out with you. And if we give up, we lose that, and . . . and we get bodysnatched by alien slugs! I'm the most scared of all of you, but I think we have to carry on.'

The silence returned and everyone shuffled their feet, the torchlight flickering over the dirty water. 'He's right,' Alex finally agreed, scratching at his scruffy hair. 'We're all hungry, tired, freaked out, but we have to go on. We have to –'

He didn't get to finish his sentence. A piercing shriek killed the words in his throat, coming from Oli.

'What is it?' gasped Mo, shining his torch at him.

'My . . . my arm,' Oli managed to get out, frozen, his eyes as wide as saucers. 'There's something crawling up my arm!'

The terror in his voice made everyone stumble backwards. Mo's breath caught as he saw a small black shape wriggling along Oli's sleeve.

'It's a slug thing,' he hissed. 'One of those freaky nose-climber ones!'

Oli broke through his paralysis and he yelped in fear and disgust as he flicked the creature off so that it splatted on the tunnel wall.

'There's another one too, just up ahead at the junction!' announced Riley, pointing with her torch.

'Look,' said Sophia, a touch of hope returning to her voice as she aimed her beam further ahead. 'There's a whole load of them.'

'What do we do?' asked Oli, grabbing a piece of metal pipe that lay in the water by his feet. 'Squish them all?'

'No,' answered Alex decisively. 'We follow them.'

Mo was glad he'd taken a stand, but he was relieved he was no longer in charge.

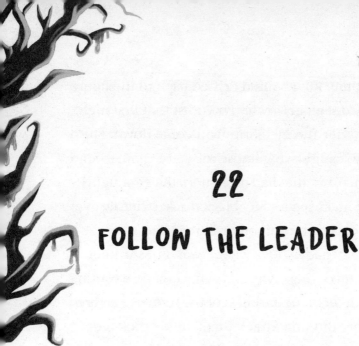

22

FOLLOW THE LEADER

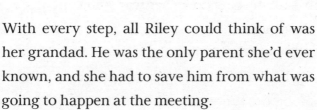

With every step, all Riley could think of was her grandad. He was the only parent she'd ever known, and she had to save him from what was going to happen at the meeting.

And that meant the invention that clunked away in her backpack had to work.

The five of them trudged on, slowly now, like soldiers on a secret mission, edging along behind the slugs. Riley would have gone down into the sewers on her own if the others had refused, but she was very glad they'd all agreed to come along.

As they crept onwards, more slugs joined the procession up ahead, like some weird convoy of slime. Riley's mind drifted back to the figure they'd seen in Howlmoor Forest that first night, just after the meteorite had come down. She'd only caught a glimpse of it, a split-second glance, but that had been more than enough. Its face had been a slimy black mask, two pale eyes burning out from somewhere inside.

Riley had no idea what it was, but she knew it was terrifying. Was that same creature waiting for them in the darkness of the tunnels, ready to spring out and attack them? Riley took a deep breath, forcing down her fear, and kept up with the others.

It was Oli that heard the sound first. He held up his hand, a finger to his lips, and pointed along the tunnel. Everyone froze, and that was when Riley heard it too. Words, a clamour of voices, coming from just above their heads.

'Listen,' hissed Alex. 'There's people up there.'

Riley paused for a moment, trying to block out the sound of the drips and the running water and the echoes of the town above, focusing on the babble of conversation from somewhere nearby.

'Look!' whispered Mo, pointing at a grille that led up to the outside world. Riley took a step closer, peering through the drain to the street above them. A succession of feet trampled past.

'We must be near the town hall,' said Oli, elbowing his way in next to Riley. 'They're probably all heading to the meeting.'

'That means we're close,' exclaimed Sophia.

'And it also means we don't have long,' warned Riley, turning to set off after the slugs once more.

'Wait,' hissed Oli. 'Look who it is!'

The tone of Oli's voice made Riley move back towards the drain. Through the gap, she saw Bethany Blight and her parents, swept along in the crowd. Riley caught a snippet of their conversation, drifting down through the drain.

'– don't even want to go. I could be at home, watching television or doing my homework,' came Bethany's sulky voice.

'Making someone's life a misery, more like,' muttered Mo. 'You know what, I've changed my mind. If Bethany's heading to the town hall, I think we should let those slugs have her.'

'Tempting,' agreed Riley. 'But saving Bethany is a price worth paying to stop anyone else getting hurt. And whether we make it out of this or not, she's not going to bully you any more. You've got us now. Come on.'

They set off into the darkness again, the voices from above fading as the tunnel they were in started to slope, heading deeper underground.

'I don't like this,' breathed Mo.

'Up ahead,' warned Alex a few seconds later. 'The tunnel widens, and there's something else, some weird kind of sound.'

Riley heard it too, a deep rumbling like distant thunder, making the skin on her arms turn to gooseflesh. She lifted her newest invention, took a deep breath and slid her finger over the trigger.

23
MONSTERS

Alex had never believed in monsters.

From as far back as he could remember, he'd thought that strange events could always be explained, and that there certainly, most definitely, was no such thing as monsters.

But when he finally saw what was lurking in the sewers deep beneath Shiver Point, Alex realised he'd been wrong. Very, very wrong.

The chamber where the tunnels met and where the slugs had converged was large and circular, like a metallic goldfish bowl buried far under the ground. Five tunnels branched off from the chamber, leading towards different parts of the town.

It wasn't the tunnels though that had caught Alex's eye.

It was the thing that hung from the ceiling.

Long strands of black slime stretched from the walls and the roof to make a huge spiderweb of goo, like a safety net full of gunk and litter, up above their heads. And what lay in the centre of the web was even worse.

When Alex had seen the creature before, among the trees of the forest and then through his own bedroom window late at night, he hadn't got a proper look, just brief glimpses of something that seemed too awful to be real. But now, by the light of their torches, he saw everything a little too clearly.

The creature resembled a human in form, only it was far taller and coated in a thick layer of slime. Its skeletal limbs were curled up into a ball, the spider at the centre of the web, and a steady procession of slugs was slithering up and down the strands. Everything about the creature seemed strange and menacing – the misshapen bulge of its head, the long spindly fingers that ended in vicious talons. Where its face should have been there was just a black void, and Alex's brain flashed back to that first night in the forest, those terrifying eyes and teeth he'd glimpsed through the shadows.

'I think . . . I think it's asleep,' he heard himself whisper.

'That would make sense,' breathed Sophia. 'If it only comes out at night, maybe it sleeps all day.'

'But there isn't much day left,' Mo blurted, staring desperately at the others.

Alex couldn't take his eyes off the creature. With every breath that strange, deep rumbling filled the chamber as the creature's mouth opened and a flurry of slugs slithered out, crawling along the dark strands of slime that held the web above their heads and wriggling towards the tunnels.

'The ones that are coming back, maybe they're giving it information, telling it what they've seen,' Sophia mused, staring in awe at the thing in the web. 'And the others . . .'

'I guess they're heading off to the town hall,' Oli whispered, for once too scared to crack any jokes. Here and there, empty cans of cat food littered the chamber's floor.

'It's nearly time,' urged Mo. 'We need to –'

Riley was a step ahead, aiming her new contraption at the sleeping creature, her finger poised on the trigger.

'Wait!' hissed Sophia, jabbing her own finger towards a mass of shadows. 'What . . . what is *that*?'

On the other side of the chamber, a series of wires and leads snaked towards a large clunky machine, a mass of blinking lights and jagged circuit boards.

'What do you think, Dyson?' Oli asked, directing his question towards Riley.

Riley took a step closer, shining her torch over the strange machinery. 'It looks like it's made up of all the stuff that was stolen from the school computers. There's a load of networking parts in there . . .'

She shook her head, turning back towards the others. 'I don't know for sure, but I think it's some kind of communication device, a giant radio maybe. It might be the interference from this that's blocking the phones and internet.'

'What's it for though?' asked Alex, not sure if he really wanted to know the answer.

'My best guess . . .' Riley said, fixing her torch on the flashing lights. 'Calling someone.'

'What, like ET, phoning home?' Oli asked. 'But why?'

'To tell them about all the tasty snacks on Earth, maybe?' Mo suggested. 'Hey, everyone, it's a like a huge KFC bargain bucket down here.'

Oli rubbed longingly at his tummy. 'Can we not mention KFC right now?'

Sophia turned to him in amazement. 'How can you be hungry at a time like this?!'

Oli shrugged. 'Fear makes me hungry.'

'What do we do?' asked Alex, looking from the sleeping creature back to the strange machine. 'I mean, how about if we smash that thing and –'

'*Walk away!*' ordered a voice from behind them. 'Walk away and don't touch a thing.'

The group turned as one. Someone stood in the shadows, just outside the circle of torchlight. There was something familiar about the shape and the voice, Alex reckoned, something that told him who it was before he saw their face.

His mum.

Except he was pretty sure she wasn't quite herself any more.

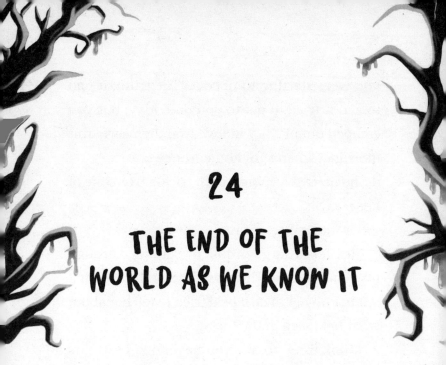

24

THE END OF THE WORLD AS WE KNOW IT

'Mum,' he exclaimed, taking a step towards her. 'What are you . . . ?'

But Alex had already guessed the answer and didn't need to finish the question. As he got closer he realised it was there, in the red-rimmed eyes, the bubbling breath, the way she didn't smile when she saw him.

'It's been watching you for nearly two weeks,' his mum explained in a cold monotone. 'You, and Mo, and Oli, and Riley, and Sophia. It saw you that first night in the forest, and it's watched you ever since. It sees what its hosts see, and it knew that you'd seen it, and when it realised you were starting to uncover the truth, it had to act. It tried to get to you on Friday, but you escaped out of the window. And then early this morning, when I got home from work . . .'

She paused, wiping a dark trickle from one of her nostrils.

'It sent its slugs for me.'

Alex felt a surge of horror running through his veins like ice. This was *his* fault. If he hadn't left her on her own, if he'd tried to tell her about what he'd seen in the forest . . .

'Mum, listen to me, you have to fight it! You have to –'

Before Alex could finish his sentence, his mum's eyes went black, as if someone had flicked a switch. When she spoke again, it wasn't her voice that came out, but a harsh, strangled sound that belonged to something else.

'You can't reason with her,' barked the words, in a tone like nails down a blackboard. 'She belongs to *me*.'

Mo pointed his torch back up towards the creature hanging above them. It was moving, stirring, the pale eyes behind the mask of black slime slowly opening.

They were running out of time.

'What do you want?' Sophia shouted up at the dark silhouette.

'Tonight this town will be mine,' Alex's mum answered in the voice that wasn't her own. 'After the meeting I will send a message up to the stars, signalling for more of my kind to come here. To *feed*.'

'Shiver Point really isn't all that tasty,' Oli protested, his voice shaking.

Beside him, Mo raised a trembling hand, polite even under such terrifying circumstances. 'Why . . . why do you want the children?' he asked.

'The adults will serve us. The flesh of the children will sustain us,' came the voice again.

'Sus-what?' asked Oli.

'It means *eat*!' snapped Sophia, moving away from the creature. Its eyes were open now, its body slowly uncoiling in its lair, a cold smile visible behind the tendrils of slime.

'The blood of human children holds the key to immortality for my kind,' came the voice again. 'And minutes from now, when the meeting starts just above our heads, I will take the rest of the adults and start to prepare the children for my people to feast on.'

Riley lifted the weird rectangular box she was holding, pointing it towards the creature. 'I've got some bad news,' she shouted, finally squeezing the trigger. 'Dinner's cancelled!'

And she kicked their plan into action.

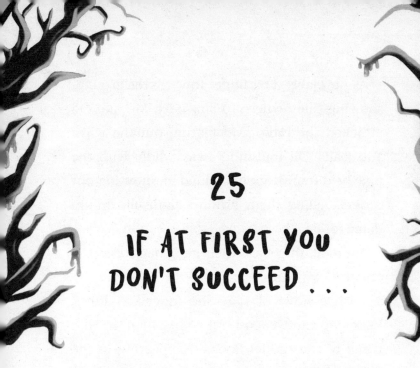

25

IF AT FIRST YOU DON'T SUCCEED . . .

Alex knew exactly what the machine in Riley's hands was, but even so he wasn't prepared for what happened next.

A dazzling beam of light shot out from the LED bulbs in the homemade UV gun, a blast of power that Riley had explained would be twice as intense as the midday sun. Suddenly the shadows of the sewers were banished, the chamber brought alive as the ray of light struck the creature, setting it ablaze and sending it tumbling from its web to land with a splash in the putrid water below.

'There! It's there!'

As Alex jabbed his finger towards the ground, showing Riley where to aim next, Mo and Oli attacked the radio, Mo tearing out the wires and leads, Oli smashing away wildly with the pipe he'd found. Sophia joined in, shouting out orders, telling them how to cause maximum damage.

But in all the chaos their gang had forgotten about Alex's mum.

With a howl of rage she lunged at Riley, knocking the weapon out of her hand so that it fell to the tunnel floor, disappearing in the water. Riley scrabbled under the surface, retrieving the machine and hitting the trigger once more.

But this time nothing happened.

'The bulbs, they're smashed!' she cried in despair.

In the far corner of the chamber, under the tattered strands of its web, the creature rose from the water, a look of fury and hatred in its pale eyes. Its whole left side was charred and burnt from where Riley's light had struck it, smoke rising from the wounds, revealing glimpses of a dark skeleton underneath.

'We need to go,' squealed Mo, backing away. 'We need to go *right now!*'

An awful shriek filled the air, rage personified, as the creature lifted one trembling clawed fingertip and pointed it in the gang's direction.

'But my mum . . .' Alex protested, staring at the motionless figure of his mother, who stood there like a robot whose power had suddenly failed. 'I can't just –'

Riley reached out, taking his hand. 'You can't help her here!' she yelled. 'If we can get her outside, into the sunlight, we hopefully can. But not if that thing gets us first!'

Alex did as he was told. With one final look back, he followed the others as they scrambled out of the chamber, the creature's howls filling their ears, just like that first night in the forest.

Sophia led the way, getting soaked by the filthy water as she ran, the furious roars of the creature behind them as it gave chase.

They reached a junction, Oli stumbling ahead of her to frantically look left and right. 'Where are we going?' he demanded.

'I don't know,' Sophia burbled back. 'As far away from here as we can!'

Alex grabbed hold of Sophia and pointed at the two tunnels.

'Shadow Hill cemetery,' he yelled. 'Which way to the bell tower there?'

Sophia's eyes narrowed, her fear replaced by confusion. 'Why would we want to go there?'

'I've got a plan B,' Alex announced, glancing back over his shoulder. 'You have to trust me on this! We need it to follow us there.'

Sophia nodded, closing her eyes for a moment as she tried to figure out where they needed to go next. A heartbeat later her eyes flew open.

'My best hunch is it's that way,' she answered, pointing to the left.

'Your best hunch?' Alex repeated. 'Based on what?'

Sophia shrugged. 'Based on the compass I have in my head. But isn't a fifty per cent chance better than none at all? Come on!'

The rest of the group followed her without question, stumbling, tripping, helping each other up when they fell. They were soggy, dirty and exhausted, but there was no way they could stop now, with the creature hot on their tails and getting closer by the second on its powerful bony legs. Their torch beams bounced off the walls and ceiling, their frantic breaths echoing down the tunnels.

'That thing *really* wants to eat us,' yelled Mo, 'so I hope you know what you're doing, Alex!'

'There,' replied Sophia, gesturing towards a jagged shape up ahead, a barred rusty gate that Alex reckoned must have been there since the tunnels were built. Oli reached it first, waiting until the others were through and then slamming it shut, the ancient hinges squealing in protest. Mo shone his torch behind them, illuminating the face of the creature that surged after them, jaws wide with fury, dozens of razor-sharp teeth ready to tear into their flesh.

Oli still had hold of the metal pipe, and he jammed it into the lock, closing the gate so that it couldn't be opened from the other side. The creature hit it like a freight train, rattling the gate on its hinges, but the barrier held firm.

'That should hold it for a few minutes at least,' breathed Riley, gasping with exhaustion. 'But what's this plan B that –'

A strange, bubbling sound cut her off, and Alex watched in horror as the figure on the other side of the bars started to change and elongate, its slimy form stretching and morphing. A moment later it started to slip through the bars of the gate, squeezing through the gaps as if it was made of black jelly.

'At least we've figured out how it got into Alex's house,' choked Sophia, watching in horror as their pursuer slowly pushed its way through.

'I know we want it to follow us,' panted Mo. 'But couldn't it let us rest for just a few seconds first?'

'Come on!' yelled Alex, dragging Mo along the tunnel. 'Run! We need to get to the bell tower before the sun sets!'

26
PLAN B

Shiver Point was deserted, the streets silent and ghostly, as if the whole town was in hibernation.

Unfortunately Alex didn't have time to enjoy the tranquillity of the scene.

He slammed the manhole cover to one side, scrambled out into the open and helped the others through one by one. After almost two hours in the sewers, they looked like zombies, their faces dark, their clothes ripped and stinking.

'Where are we?' demanded Mo, rubbing his eyes against the dim dusk light. 'Where have we come up?'

Alex looked around, trying to get his bearings.

'Over there!' shouted Riley. 'That's my house over there, that's Shadow Hill cemetery, and there's the bell tower!'

She pointed to the old stone chapel, set at the top of the hill. Alex looked towards the distant trees, spotting the sun that was just starting to disappear behind the horizon.

'We don't have long!' he yelled. 'Come on!'

Oli slammed the manhole cover back down, even though it clearly wouldn't hold their pursuer for long. But Alex was counting on that.

They began the climb towards the chapel, trampling on the fallen leaves and conkers that lined the road. Alex swung open the wrought-iron gate that led into the cemetery and sprinted up the path, checking the others were behind him. As he spun round, a huge crash shattered the calm, and he watched the manhole cover topple to one side. A moment later a dark skeletal figure clambered out into the open, steam rising from its burnt skin, hatred shining in its eyes.

'It's coming!' stammered Mo. 'Go, go, go!'

They ran up to the summit of the hill, closing in on the entrance to the chapel, the whole of Shiver Point spread out below them like a map made real. Shadow Hill was the highest point for miles, and it gave a bird's-eye view of the surrounding landscape. Alex scrambled to a stop at the doorway, staring at the different landmarks, the tall finger of Point Lighthouse, the huge stone columns of the town hall, the dark mass of Howlmoor Forest where all of this had started. Alex realised with a jolt of fear that if his plan didn't work, he'd never see the town again. He was surprised to find how much the thought upset him. At some point over the past few days, Shiver Point had become his home.

From behind him, Alex heard Riley rattle the doors, a moan of frustration slipping from her lips. 'Someone's bolted it!'

Oli pushed past her, kicking open the wooden door and beckoning them all inside. The alien was on the path now, scrambling towards the chapel, its furious howls echoing among the tombstones.

Alex's breath was a hot spike in his chest, but he forced himself on past the empty pews and the altar, towards the staircase at the front. He led the others up the stone steps, trying not to trip and fall as he heard the doors smash open and an angry roar shatter the deathly silence.

The creature had them cornered.

And if plan B didn't work, it was all over.

It only took Alex a few seconds to climb the steps, turn right, and push his way through a wooden door into the bell tower high above Shiver Point. A huge steel bell hung in the middle of the room, a pair of wooden shutters hiding the only window from view. Just next to the shutters stood a long, tall mirror, heavy enough that carrying it up here earlier had nearly broken Alex's back.

Riley and the others stumbled into the room, looking anxiously behind them towards the stairs.

'Quick,' gasped Mo. 'Whatever this plan B of yours is, you need to tell us! That thing's coming!'

Alex took a deep breath, praying that what he'd put in place earlier, when he told them all he was going to leave a note for his mum, was going to work. If it didn't, he'd put his mum at risk for nothing. He quickly explained his plan, the others listening intently for a few seconds before bursting into action.

Footsteps sounded outside the door, the alien's growl so close it was almost deafening.

A heartbeat later the creature lurched inside.

Its spindly arms were so long they dragged on the floor, sharp claws twitching hungrily. Its left side, where Riley had burned it with the UV rays, still bubbled and smoked. As it jerked into the room, Alex noticed a small dark slug wriggle out of the slime that coated it and start to slither towards them.

'Now!' he screamed, staggering backwards as the creature charged towards him.

Nobody needed telling twice. Mo slammed the door to, dropping the bolt so that the alien couldn't get out, Riley moved the mirror to the right a fraction, and Sophia and Oli wrenched open the shutters.

And the light flooded in.

The dying sun had almost sunk below the horizon, but it was still enough to thrust their plan into action. The rays hit the mirror and then reflected brightly across the room, surging against the giant metal bell. The alien froze as the resulting orange glow bathed it from head to toe in pure sunlight. Then it started to shriek and wail, its slime layer sizzling and dissolving until it revealed the thin, ebony skeleton underneath. Alex squinted against the glare, watching the creature's bones start to crumble as the light touched them. The alien writhed and struggled, one clawed hand thrashing out to crack the mirror's glass, but there was nowhere for it to run.

In less than a minute it was over.

What was left of the creature lay in a small, bubbling pile on the stone floor, a column of dark smoke rising from the remains. One last, bloated slug wriggled out from the mess, and Mo darted forward and trod on it with a loud squelch.

'We . . . we did it,' whispered Alex, not quite believing what he was seeing.

'Yeah,' Oli agreed breathlessly. 'We saved Shiver Point, didn't we? I mean, *us*. Who would ever believe it?!'

Sophia plodded towards the mirror, staring at the broken glass. 'Seven years bad luck,' she mumbled. 'As if we need any more of that.'

Somewhere in the distant night, sirens howled, coming closer. Alex looked towards the window, just in time to see the last glimmer of the sun's rays disappear behind the trees.

'We need to leave,' Riley announced, cocking her head to the side. 'If they find that broken door downstairs, we're in *big* trouble.'

Oli gave a heavy nod. 'Home or the treehouse?'

'I need to go back down into the sewers,' Alex said, 'and find my mum. Hopefully she's woken up, just like the police officer did.'

'We'll come with you,' Sophia said, and Mo, Riley and Oli all nodded their agreement.

Alex took one last look at the pool of black slime on his way out – the only proof that the creature from the woods had ever existed at all.

THE SHIVERING POST

Mysterious amnesia rocks Shiver Point!

Reported by Damian Thorn

Shiver Point's doctors have been inundated with calls from dozens of residents who claim to have suffered from an unknown virus that made them completely forget the events of the previous forty-eight hours. The strange symptoms were first reported on Sunday night, just before the town meeting, when Shiver Point Mayor David Drake was about to go on stage, only to forget what he was going to say and where he was. The mayor's distress was swiftly shared by several other residents reporting the same curious ailment, leading to the cancellation of the town meeting.

Dr Gemma Sampson, Shiver Point's leading doctor, tried to reassure residents with the following diagnosis: 'It's an unusual set of symptoms, but I don't think it's anything to be overly worried about. Each of the patients I've spoken to had a strange, chesty cough, accompanied by a rather disgusting runny black mucus which seems to be connected to the amnesia. All of them can remember long-term events, but not the incidents of the past few days, so there's no sign of any lasting damage.'

According to police reports, several people woke up from the amnesia to find themselves in a variety of unusual locations, including in the sewer system and Howlmoor Forest. Some residents also reported that their cupboards were full of cat food, although they don't own a cat and have no idea how it could have got there.

With all the concerns about the strange amnesia, the recent string of disturbing events in the town have faded into the background. Apart from signs of a break-in at the chapel at Shadow Hill cemetery, no other incidents have been reported, and with phone and internet services to the town restored, it seems that life in Shiver Point is returning to normal.

EPILOGUE

ENDINGS AND BEGINNINGS

It had been two weeks since the day Alex and the others had fought the creature that fell into Howlmoor, and life in Shiver Point was gradually getting back to normal.

Which for Alex meant kind of boring.

And a little lonely too.

He hadn't seen much of the rest of the gang, on account of everyone wanting to spend as much time with their families as possible. The walkie-talkie Riley had given to Alex sat gathering dust on his bedside table, not a single word hissing over the airwaves. Of course, Alex had spotted the others around school, but things felt different.

In a way, it was as if a spell had been in place, binding their little group together, but now the alien was dead, the magic bond had broken.

Alex was rolling back and forth on the halfpipe, practising his kick turns, when his mum joined him. She had her nurse's uniform on as usual at this time, but there was something different about her tonight, something Alex couldn't quite put his finger on.

'You had a visitor earlier when you were out doing my shopping,' she announced, a playful smile on her lips.

'Who was it?'

The smile grew. 'A girl. Kind of quirky. Pretty. Seemed cool. Said her name was Riley.'

The words made Alex almost fall off his board. 'What did she want?'

'She wanted to know if you were around. When I said you weren't home, she asked me to let you know she'd like you to go over to hers, if you fancy it.'

'OK,' managed Alex, trying to keep his voice as neutral as he could.

His mum waited for a little more information, glancing at her watch impatiently before caving in with a sigh. 'So are you going to? Go over to her house, I mean?'

Alex weighed the question up in his mind, picturing the life he'd had before Shiver Point came into it, the friends he'd been forced to leave behind.

'I don't know.'

The wooden ramp creaked as his mum sat down beside him.

'I've got some other news,' she said, staring out at the pines that stood tall in the sinking sun. 'Something you might be glad to hear. This is the last time I'm going to be leaving for work at night.'

Alex cocked his head to one side. 'Seriously?'

'Yep. That weird virus I had last week, all the stuff I couldn't remember, it just made me think about how hard I've been working and how I've been missing out on time with you.'

Alex felt his breath catch at the words. For a heartbeat he was back in the sewers, just minutes after the events in the chapel, finding his mum stumbling around in the dark, dazed and confused. Oli had been right after all – if the alien was the big boss, killing it had done the same to its weird slug offspring, allowing their hosts to regain control of their bodies.

'Before I know it,' his mum continued, bringing Alex back to the present, 'you'll be buying a car, then you'll be off to college, and I'll never see you.'

Alex laughed. 'Mum, I'm twelve.'

His mum looked down, fiddling with the name badge on her scrubs. 'I know. But I've asked my manager to take me off the late shifts. And I told them no more working so much overtime too. It's the least they can do after transferring me here.'

She paused, a wry smile lighting up her face. 'Also, I'm not sure Alison is the *most* effective of childminders.'

Alex glanced towards Alison's house next door. Like his mum, she seemed her usual self again now that things in the town were back to normal. Earlier that day, Alex had seen her fast asleep in the rocking chair on her front porch, despite the fact that a group of maintenance workers were loudly drilling up the road.

His mum rose up from the ramp, her face serious again. 'I know you don't love it here, and you miss home and your old friends, but I hope we can make it work. And I'll do whatever I can to make it easier.'

Alex pictured his old friends, but their faces seemed distant and blurry now. Instead, he found himself thinking of Riley and the others.

Maybe his mum was right. Maybe things *could* work here.

'But tonight I still have to go to work,' his mum continued. 'So do something for me, will you?'

Alex stared up at her. 'What?'

'Go and see this Riley. Give your friends here a chance. Sometimes you just need to take a gamble.'

Seeing Riley's treehouse again gave Alex a strange twist of nerves in his tummy. The fairy lights were on, and the treehouse seemed to glow and shimmer in the dusk. Only now that they didn't have the town to save, he wasn't sure what he and the others had in common any more.

Riley climbed down the rope ladder just as Alex reached the base of the tree.

'You ignoring us?' she called as she hit the ground.

'Nah, I just . . . I didn't know what to say.'

Riley shivered as the wind blew, wrapping her arms around herself. 'I get it. How's your mum doing?'

For a moment Alex was back in the sewers, his mum speaking in a voice that wasn't her own. He swallowed, doing his best to force the image out of his brain.

'She's good. Doesn't remember much apart from waking up in the sewers and having no idea how she got there, but that's definitely for the best. Although she has developed a bit of a taste for cat food ...'

Riley laughed, the sound warm and happy. 'You're not serious?'

Alex grinned, and he thought maybe it was the first genuine smile he'd had since arriving in Shiver Point. 'Yeah. She wasn't best pleased about her missing mirror either.'

Riley laughed again.

Raised voices sounded from above them, ones that Alex knew a little too well.

'Mo's here, and Oli, and Sophia,' Riley explained. 'Want to come up?'

Alex took a deep breath, staring up at the treehouse. He wanted to say yes, but what if he and his mum moved on again? What if he made friends and lost them just like before?

Take a gamble, urged his mum's voice, deep inside his brain.

Alex opened his mouth to reply, but a voice from above beat him to it. 'What are you two doing down there? Kissing?'

Alex felt colour rush to his cheeks.

'No!' yelled Riley. 'No way! We're just talking.'

Oli's head poked out of the treehouse door, a mischievous gap-toothed grin on his face. 'What about? *Love?*'

Alex grabbed a pine cone from the leaves by his feet and hurled it at Oli. Oli disappeared, and when he reappeared Sophia and Mo were alongside him.

'Hey, Alex,' called Mo. 'Did Riley ask you?'

'Ask me what?'

'About the gang, of course,' shouted Sophia, her school uniform washed clean from all the sewer dirt and as neat as ever. Even if it was a weekend.

Alex turned to find Riley's dark eyes boring into him. 'Gang?'

Riley shrugged. 'We're thinking of forming a little crew. Who knows, Shiver Point might need us again one day. After all, we did save the town, even if no one else will ever know.'

Mo, Oli and Sophia stared down at Alex expectantly.

'So what's it called?' Alex asked. 'Geeks R Us? Nerds Direct?'

Riley shook her head, a playful smile on her lips. 'I think we're a little cleverer than Bethany Blight, don't you? We were thinking of calling it the Shiver Squad.'

Alex laughed, the cold air biting into his lungs. 'I like it.'

Riley pulled out her mobile phone, typed away at it for a second and then held the screen up for Alex to see.

'We've set up our own group chat, so if there's ever another situation we can spread the word straight away.'

She took a step backwards, jabbing her thumb towards the treehouse. 'So what do you think? Want to join?'

Riley has added Alex to 'SHIVER SQUAD'

GET READY FOR THE SHIVER
SQUAD'S NEXT TERRIFYING
MYSTERY ...

CREEPING ONTO BOOKSHELVES SOON!

ABOUT THE AUTHOR

After discovering an anthology of horror stories lurking in the library of his primary school, Gabriel fell in love with all things frightening and creepy.

It Came From the Woods is the first chilling instalment in Shiver Point, a new middle-grade series from Piccadilly Press. Mixing scares with humour, it references Gabriel's love of classic horror films from the eighties and nineties and includes many of the creatures that scare him the most.

When not writing books intended to frighten tweens and teens, Gabriel is a keen surfer and snowboarder. He lives in the south-west of England with his wife and three young children.

We hope you loved your Piccadilly Press book!

For all the latest bookish news, freebies and exclusive content, sign up to the Piccadilly Press newsletter – scan the QR code or visit lnk.to/PiccadillyNewsletter

Follow us on social media:

bonnierbooks.co.uk/PiccadillyPress